THE UNHALLOWED

THE WITCH HUNTER SAGA - BOOK FIVE

NICOLE R. TAYLOR

PROLOGUE

Nye Saer leaned against the fence outside of York Minster, watching the stream of nobles done up in their winter finery enter the church for Sunday mass. The cathedral spire towered into the mist, the tip vanishing into the dense fog, but it only reminded him of the spectre he'd become.

In the distance, he could see a group of peasants trudging through the mud, all of them making their way toward the smaller church on the edge of town past the green. York Minster was reserved for those with titles and wealth, no matter the doctrine of God.

"My lord, the service starts soon."

He glanced up to see his faithful companion, Lewes, wringing his hands together nervously. He was only faithful because he made him that way. He had neither the time nor the inclination to win him over the right way, so he compelled the man to give him a friendly helping hand.

"I care not," he replied. "I don't believe in your God, Lewes. He wasn't around to save me when I needed saving."

He'd been a vampire for thirteen miserable years. A wretched thing that clung to shadows and preyed on the unwary. He'd been a slave to the night for a decade before he even found a witch who could help him feel the sun against his dead skin once more. A decade of darkness. Not that the light had made him fare any better. There was no God. Not in his world.

For all the bad things he had been changed into, there were many good things. His body was perfect despite the scar marring his face. From the top of his right temple, across the bridge of his nose, and down his left cheek, a puckered gash severed his face, marking him as an undesirable. Unfortunate considering he'd gotten it fighting for the English Crown against the Spanish Armada some fifteen years before when he was still human. Despite his features, he was stronger than he'd ever been, faster and hardly tired at all. He was fuelled by blood and soothed by alcohol.

Casting his gaze over the fog-laden village square, he felt her coming before he even knew the direction. He'd hoped she would come today. Perhaps it was foolish considering his circumstance, but he wanted it, anyway.

Finally, she emerged from the mist, her delicate form wrapped tight in a dark cloak, her skirts trailing in the slush of last night's snowfall. He knew her name quite well. Eleanor. Eleanor, who wanted to love a vampire. She had chosen him but in her lust had neglected to tell him about her coven.

"Lewes," he said. "Go to church, and say your prayers. I will come and collect you when the sermon ends...if I am still alive to do so."

"But my lord—"

"Be gone before I make you."

Knowing what was good for him, the man scuttled away, joining the line of nobles entering the Minster.

Nye turned and watched Eleanor approach, her long, curly chestnut hair blowing in the icy wind that had picked up with her arrival. A few flakes of snow spiralled around the square, and he couldn't help marvelling at her beauty. Had he known she was a witch from the beginning, he wouldn't have touched her, but by the time she revealed herself, it was too late. He'd already had a taste of her body and didn't have the strength to turn her away.

"Nye Saer," she said, her voice sounding almost musical in the close air. "Vampires are not welcome here. You know this, yet here you remain."

"You weren't complaining last week, Eleanor."

"Things change." She traced her fingers along the edge of his cloak, her teeth tugging at her bottom lip. "You must leave or suffer the consequences."

"But you still want it," he murmured, stepping

closer. "I can hear your heart beating. No matter what they say, you still want me, Eleanor."

Her hand trailed up his collar, along his neck, into his hair, and she pulled him against her, crushing her lips with his. He had no control where she was concerned, and he kissed her back, taking her as deeply as he could in such a public place.

"Come," she whispered against his swollen mouth.

Nye felt the crackle in the air that betrayed the power in her command, but he didn't have it in him to deny her. Taking her hand, she led him from the square and through the streets until they reached the wood that bordered against the far edge of town.

"What is this?" he asked, snow crunching underfoot.

Eleanor dropped his hand and pushed him back against a tree, kissing him again. His body began to take over and he grasped her waist, spinning her around and pinning her against the trunk of the ancient oak. Something deep inside him said this was a trap. He should've known better considering in his last life he'd been a spy for the English Crown. He should've known they'd turn her against him. He didn't want to be a vampire—he was cheated by a cruel twist of fate—but a part of him loved this witch, and that was his downfall

He kissed her with all the passion he could muster, sliding his tongue against hers, showing her how much she meant to him...how much he cared for her. But it was never going to be enough. He felt the magic rising in her before he could pull away, and he knew he'd failed. She shoved him back, a look of malice etched into her beautiful features.

Gagging, he stumbled, clutching at his throat. "What have you done?"

"The Unhallowed will suffer your presence no longer." She pushed him again, and he fell backward into the snow with a thud, his movements becoming sluggish.

So they'd bade her to kill him, then. Strangely, he didn't feel that alarmed considering he was well aware of what the witches were capable of.

Eleanor straddled him, pulling out a blade and pressing it against his forehead. The sting of metal cut into him, and he hissed at her, but she ignored his pitiful wailing and continued carving his skin.

"Such an unfortunate life," she crooned, tracing his scar with the tip of her bloody blade. The stench of his own blood was overpowering, threatening to take his control, but there was nothing he could do about it.

"So much pain," she murmured. "I will take it away. I will deliver you, Nye. I promise."

She began to speak in the strange language of the witches, and the symbol she'd cut into his forehead began to sear with unbelievable agony. "*Eleanor*—"

There was a gust of wind, and suddenly, she was gone. Immediately, the burning pain stopped, and he sat up, gasping for air. Nye's gaze locked onto a tall man standing on the opposite side of the clearing, his hand curled into Eleanor's hair. She let out a whimper as he twisted his hand, a sick look of satisfaction on his face.

Nye knew the man was a vampire. He could see it in his eyes—the way the colour swirled from white into black—and in the pallor of his skin.

"You know what you need to do, brother," he said, forcing Eleanor to her knees. With his other hand, he drew a sword from under his black cloak and held it out hilt first.

Stumbling to his feet, Nye took the sword, somehow knowing it was in his best interests if he did. Hesitating, he looked down at Eleanor and saw that her eyes were full of fear. She had no issues with taking his life, but when it came to hers…

"The love you feel is false," the man said. "End her and you will end your misery."

Eleanor's eyes began to darken, her mouth twisting into a devilish smile. The air began to thicken, and he knew he was dead if he didn't do what the man bade him. They'd both die. As the words formed in her throat, he raised the sword and struck with all his supernatural strength. He hardly felt it when the blade severed flesh and bone, but he felt his heart break…or what was left of it.

The stench of blood was almost immediate as it splattered over the white snow, a stark contrast if he ever saw one. Eleanor's body dropped with a thud, the red of her life soaking into the earth. Propping himself up with the bloody sword, he covered his nose and mouth with a trembling hand to smother the scent of his dead lover.

Finally looking up at the man who'd saved him, he asked, "Who are you?"

The man smirked and dropped Eleanor's head. It landed in the snow with a dull thud as he theatrically dusted off his hands.

"I am Regulus, and I've been watching you, Nye Saer."

CHAPTER 1

Nye Saer had been through a lot in the last few weeks.

That was saying something considering all the things he'd experienced in his four hundred years as a vampire.

He sat at the rear bar of The Good Mixer—a little pub just off High Street in Camden, London—nursing a pint of the swill they deigned to call beer. Things had been crazy, battling ancient covens of witches and three-thousand-year-old fairy-vampire hybrids, and now the London vampires were without a leader, and everyone thought he was the one who could take the crown. If only it were that simple.

It was a month since his best mate, Zac Degaud, had left with the hybrid Aya to go to America, and after all they'd been through together, he was beginning to feel lonely. Ironic considering he was still stuck with Tristan, the thousand-year-old Irish vampire, and

Gabby Cohen, who was one of the most powerful witches alive.

Nye had forsaken all that he'd come to know to go against his master—the founding vampire, Regulus—to side with Zac, and now everything was in turmoil.

Regulus was a tough act to follow. He'd ruled with fear, respect, and an iron fist. Crossing him was not an option, and those who did paid in blood. Being truly immortal and able to compel vampires had been a valuable asset, but Nye had neither skill. As the leader of the Six, he'd commanded much of the same respect and fear, but he had nothing else to fall back on.

If he made a threat, he'd better be able to follow through.

Playing with his phone, he saw a text message from Tristan saying Gabby was at the Hampstead house. He worried a lot about her lately. After Regulus had died, the founder left all his earthly belongings to her, including the mansion where he'd lived a vast majority of his recent life. Time was a hard thing to fathom when one was four hundred, let alone two thousand years.

Gabby had taken Regulus's death hard and hadn't been herself since. Not that he knew her very well beforehand, but he could tell these things. A powerful witch who felt the loss of her one true love with nothing to occupy her time. It was either a recipe for disaster or nothing to worry about. He was still waiting to see which it would be.

Anyway, how a witch could fall in love with a vampire like Regulus, he'd never know.

"The Six have disbanded," he heard someone say behind him.

Straightening up slightly, Nye allowed his hearing to reach out and grasp the words of the heated conversation behind him.

"The only one left around here is Nye, and I don't know what happened to him," a second male voice said.

"What do you mean by that?"

"He changed sides, didn't he?"

"He helped that American vampire kill Regulus," another said.

"He's a spineless traitor to his own kind."

Nye tightened his grip around his pint of beer, silently seething. How was he meant to command the whole city if this is what they thought of him? Gabby thought he could do it, and Tristan was prepared to back him up as his right-hand man, but what good was it if the others didn't fall in line?

He knew they wouldn't respond to heartfelt speeches and bribery. Vampires like these would only listen to one thing. Violence.

Nye had been born a good man but had become a bad vampire given enough time. Even when he was human, he'd learned to do bad things to make the world a better place. Sometimes, doing terrible deeds was the only way to get people's attention, especially when you needed to get a point across in record time.

Nye downed the last of his beer and slammed the glass onto the bar, his fingers itching at the promise of getting dirty. He tuned out the vampires as they became rowdier in their disrespect and took a deep breath. There was one seated directly behind him with the biggest mouth of the lot. He'd called his new master spineless. Well, something could be done about that.

The moment he turned around was the moment they realised who was sitting directly behind them. There was no hiding the scar on his face—the scar that marked who he was. No, the moment he turned around was the moment he taught these insubordinates a lesson. There was a reason he became the leader of the Six, and it wasn't because of his good looks.

Luckily for him, the bar was almost empty, and since the staff was in the know about their orientation, the back was unattended. Flipping up the collar of his jacket, Nye was out of his seat. His hand curled into the vampire's hair, and a split second later, his face was hitting the tabletop with a crash. Everyone scattered, and the men that had been seated around the one with the big mouth stumbled to their feet, eyes wide with shock.

"Tell me the bit again where I'm a spineless traitor," he snarled into the vampire's ear.

"I... I..." the vampire stammered.

"*Speak up*," Nye roared into his ear. "*I can't hear you.*"

"I'm sorry!"

The way he trembled it was a wonder the asshole didn't piss his pants. This one let fear overcome everything, which made him a liability.

"Sorry isn't good enough, mate," Nye snarled, pulling the vampire to his feet while his friends stared on in silence. "Even your friends don't give a crap about saving you, so why the fuck should I let you go? Vampires like you need to be made an example of."

"Please," the vampire whimpered.

Nye let him go and stepped back, letting his gaze run over the assembled vampires. They all stood in rigid silence, waiting to see what he would do. They wanted a show and something they could use against him, and he would give them neither.

Darting forward, he grasped the smart-mouthed vampire's head and twisted. His neck snapped with an audible crack, and he fell to the ground in a heap. He was dead for now, but the guy would wake up with one hell of a headache and hurt pride. Nye would've preferred tearing his heart out and severing his spinal cord, but what point would that make? He was aiming for fear, not carnage.

Stepping over the unconscious vampire, Nye eyed the men around him with a dark expression. Without another word, he pushed the door open and left.

There was only one way he was going to continue leading this city and that was with the most powerful weapon there was. It was the same for vampires as it was humans. Fear drove men and beasts to do what they were told if it was wielded in the right manner. This was something Nye could do.

If he was ruling this city...tonight was a damn fine start.

Nye slammed the front door to Regulus's Hampstead home—he should really say it was Gabby's—and thundered up the stairs.

The walk back to the mansion and the lingering scent of blood had only served to rile him up even further. What the hell was he thinking when he agreed to this stupid charade?

Thundering up the stairs, he shoved into the study where Tristan was seated by the fireplace. The knight glanced up and eyed his stature with a raised eyebrow.

"Where have you been? You stink," he said, wrinkling his nose.

"I stink?" Nye exclaimed, pointing to himself.

"I can't leave you two alone for five seconds," Gabby said, walking into the room behind him.

Turning, Nye cast his gaze over the witch. Her brown hair was pulled back into a tight ponytail, her matching eyes sparkling. She was in a mood, and he wasn't sure if it was good or bad. She held a small leather-bound book in her hands that carried the stink of magic and age. If he wasn't mistaken, it was Katrin's grimoire.

She sat in the chair opposite Tristan by the fireplace, leaving him leaning against the desk.

"What are you doing with that?" Nye asked, nodding at the grimoire.

"I've been studying it," Gabby replied, opening the cover and running her fingers across the page.

Tristan was still staring at him, and he didn't like it when he stared. He had this thing where he didn't blink for the longest time, and that wasn't normal.

"What?" Nye snapped when he'd had enough.

The knight shrugged.

"Oh, for fuck's sake, Tristan. Just say whatever it is you've got on your mind."

"If you let them get to you, they'll see it as a weakness and keep tryin' to exploit it."

He rolled his eyes, glancing at Gabby.

"Don't look at me," she said.

"I believe this was your idea, little witch," he replied sullenly.

"You're meant to be this badass vampire, Nye," she bit back. "So be a badass vampire."

"Badass doesn't always translate."

"I'm going home to Ashburton," she said, ignoring his quip. "Alex... Alex has some loose ends to tie up, and I'm needed."

At the mention of Alex, Nye stiffened. Alex was a new vampire, and mere weeks had passed since Gabby herself turned him into a founder. He'd been used as a weapon against the insane-as-they-came fae hybrid Aed. Alex was the only vampire left on the planet who couldn't be killed by normal means. It took a special kind of magic to bring him down.

But Nye wasn't interested in Alex. The founder was on their side being that he was childhood friends with Gabby so no problems there. He was more interested in Alex's older sister, Isobel, and wanted to ask how she was doing after returning to her studies at Oxford...but he wasn't supposed to be interested. Isobel was never meant to be part of this world. Kidnapped by Aed before he and Zac could stop him, she'd already been put into more danger than he liked.

"Then go home," Nye said, putting the redhead out of his mind. "I've survived for four hundred years without you Gabby. I'll survive a few weeks more."

"Wow. That's so nice of you," she said sarcastically. "But I don't need your permission, *Your Majesty*." She flipped through the grimoire. "I'll be gone a week or so at most. Then I'll be back to assist you with bringing order to this place."

"Is that what you dragged me back here for?" Nye asked. "I was in the middle of doing just that, you know."

"No, not entirely. I need to destroy the spell that created the founders," she explained.

"And you need us here for that?" Nye asked, raising an eyebrow. "Can't you just rip out the page and throw it in the fire? Sounds easy to me."

"It doesn't work that way," Tristan said, butting in.

"A grimoire is an extension of a witch's soul in a way," Gabby went on, her fingers tracing the lines of the spell. "And when a witch casts a spell, she obtains an affinity with it. When I turned Alex…"

"It was a big deal?" Nye finished for her.

"A very big deal. When I tear this page out and burn it, I'll likely feel all of it. If it's too much, it might…" She shrugged.

"It might kill her," Tristan said.

Nye shrugged and crossed his arms over his chest. "So we give you some vampire blood before your heart stops completely."

"Hopefully, you won't have to," Gabby said, staring at the spell. "But this needs to be done. Aya is the only creature alive who can kill a founder. If something happened to her, I'm not sure nature could find a way to balance out the difference."

Nye snorted. Aya was Zac's love and was half vampire and half Celestine. The Celestines were the race that created the first witches and were all but gone, which was why they were forced to leave their magic inside a bunch of frail humans with corruptible hearts. Katrin was one of the first and hadn't been the best choice if anyone had been around to ask Nye. She'd created the founding vampires and they'd taken the last Celestine, Aya, and killed her family. The Roman founder Arturius had changed her into a vampire, not knowing what he was creating, which was the key to their demise.

For two thousand years, they'd all been embroiled in a sick, twisted game of revenge...all in the name of keeping the balance of power within the earth.

"Then rip, little witch," Nye said. "We'll be here to bring you back if you fall off the edge. Then you can go on your holiday."

Gabby squared her shoulders and picked up the edge of the page. Taking a deep breath, she closed her eyes and ripped. A gasp escaped her lips as the paper tore, her heartbeat quickening as pain flowed through her body. Nye listened and waited as she held the spell in her trembling fingers.

"Shit," she cursed.

"Okay?" Tristan asked, leaning forward.

"It was worse than I thought..." She swallowed hard but didn't back down from her duty.

Closing the grimoire, she placed it on the side table and held the page out toward the fire. Holding steady, she sucked in her deepest breath yet and let the page flutter into the flames.

The moment the two elements connected, Gabby let out an agonised wail and fell forward. Nye sprang into action and caught her in his arms before she had a chance to hit the floor.

Glancing at Tristan as she writhed in his arms, the

knight frowned, but there was nothing they could do until the fire had erased all trace of the spell. Why witches always had to do things the hard way never failed to confuse the hell out of him.

His gaze flickered to the fire where the spell was smouldering into ash, and as his keen vampire eyes observed the last of the magic fading away, Gabby began to settle. Her heartbeat had accelerated but never slowed, not until the pain was leaving her body. Either the spell wasn't as powerful as she first thought or she had more power than any of them knew.

"I'm okay," she finally whispered, her voice wavering. "I'm okay."

"Shit," Nye said, helping her back into the chair. "You witches are a morbid lot."

"Me? Morbid?" she asked, swatting him on the shoulder. "Says the vampire who drinks human blood to survive."

He smirked, trying to hide the fact that he actually liked Gabby. A lot. Vampires and witches were meant to be mortal enemies given their beginnings. It was the dawning of a new age in more ways than one.

"Point well made," he said, ignoring Tristan's chuckle in the background. "Death becomes me, right?"

"Still a smartass," Gabby murmured, looking tired.

"And I'll still be the smartest ass of the lot when you get back."

"Thank you, Nye."

CHAPTER 2

The mansion was quiet without Gabby within its walls.

Nye leaned back in the chair behind the desk in the study, stabbing a gold letter opener into the mahogany. A million and one problems to deal with and no discernible way to begin tackling them.

Outside, night had fallen, the air had taken on iciness, and the witching hour was upon the city. Trouble was brewing—he could feel it in every breath he took—but he wasn't sure where it was coming from first.

Tristan appeared in the doorway in all his curly-haired Irish glory, and Nye glanced up at the knight. He had better have good news or at least a lead on someone he could kill. It was far too long since he had the pleasure of dealing the ultimate punishment.

"What are you doing?" Tristan asked, watching the trajectory of the letter opener.

"Stabbing shit," Nye replied, rolling his eyes. "What do you want?"

"There's a prize fighter who's stirring up trouble," Tristan replied, getting right to the point. "Hate speech, anti-witch..."

"Anti-Nye," Nye spat. "I know what they say about me, Tristan. I'm a spineless witch lover. Traitor to his own kind. I did conspire to kill Regulus, after all."

He and Zac had killed the Roman, but Gabby had tricked them into believing the deed had actually been done. Zac had been prepared to die, knowing that if he took the founder's life, he'd bite the dust along with him. Gabby had put a stop to that, not knowing the founder was the only creature who could end a larger threat, which was crazyass vampire-fairy hybrids. It wasn't until Aed had bitten the founder that he actually kicked the bucket, but Nye would never live down the fact he'd been a part of the conspiracy.

Regulus had been respected, and Nye...well, apparently, he was a spineless witch-loving traitor if the rumours were to be believed.

"I think we should do somethin' about him before it gets out of control," Tristan said, eyeing him.

Nye's fingers tightened around the letter opener. "And what would you have me do?"

"That's not for me to decide," the knight went on. "You're the leader here, Nye. Not me. I agreed to be here to help, not use you like a puppet."

Nye scowled and imbedded the letter opener into

the surface of the desk, the gold blade sinking deep into the mahogany. Things had been so easy when he only had the Six to worry about. Orders were handed down. He made sure they were carried out, and he was congratulated on a job well done. Now he had to compile those orders and gather his own followers to hand them to.

Snorting, he straightened up in the chair and smoothed down his black shirt. There was only one thing he could do in this situation.

Glancing at Tristan, he said, "Let's go pay him a visit he'll never forget."

The city was buzzing as they ventured through the darkened streets to the warehouse, which sat just off Old Street in Hoxton.

The building had been spelled a long time ago by an unknown witch to be negligible to humans, which was a juxtaposition considering vampires weren't meant to take favours from their kind. Nye didn't know who had originally set this place up or why, but nothing about it pointed to the fact the spell was consented to. Most likely, it was under duress.

The man on the door was the usual stock standard security thug. He was a six foot five, bald, mean-looking son of a bitch who looked like he delighted in dishing out punishment. Not of the kind they'd find inside...no, more like a tiny power trip that made men like these think their pitiful lives were worth living.

Nye knew the guy was a vampire, he had to be considering the patrons he let in and out all night, and as they sauntered down the lane, the stench of blood and sweat began to seep through the cracks around him.

The bouncer's eyes widened as he recognised the two vampires, and he began to back away. Nye nodded toward him, and Tristan sprang into action, moving forward silently.

Pushing the oversized man against the wall, the knight said, "You didn't see us, understand? If your mouth so much as opens, I'll remove your tongue and shove it up your ass."

"Very dignified," Nye drawled.

"Vampires like him love to lick ass to get ahead," Tristan replied, still holding the bouncer in place. "Seems like he understands, yes?"

Nye looked the guy up and down and could smell his fear mixed with the delightful scent wafting out the door. Patting him on the shoulder, he smiled condescendingly. "There's a good boy," he said. "Keep your mouth shut, and you'll get a good show tonight."

He nodded, his head bobbing up and down eagerly. "Yes, sir."

"See, Tristan?" Nye said as they walked into the warehouse. "Fear is a wonderful tool when death is a normal part of everyday life. We may live a long time, but it means little when it can be taken away with a flick of the wrist."

"Much like a human life," the knight replied.

Nye snorted. "Enough philosophy. I want to see what this fighter is preaching to these imbeciles."

Keeping to the darkness, Nye averted his face as they moved among the crowd of vampires assembled to watch the fights that would be taking place tonight. Right now, he was the most recognisable member of the London underworld with his roguish good looks. His face was certainly a sight to behold.

Before things went tits up after he'd sided with Zac, the one-time member of the Six Maddox had fought here. Nye's lip curled as memories of Zac punching on with the vampire came to mind. Beating them at their own game was the only way to win allegiance with men like these.

"There," Tristan murmured, nodding across the room.

Nye followed the knight's gaze, finding a group of men huddled around a makeshift table that had been assembled out of wooden pallets and crates. Bottles of alcohol in various stages of completion littered the surface as their voices carried through the other groups of vampires present.

One man was becoming more passionate as their conversation progressed, his eyes wild with passion.

"He will drive us to ruin," he was saying. "Siding with witches and allowing them into Regulus's home.

Taking advice from them." Regulus had fallen in love with the witch he was so against, but he wasn't to know that. "What has he done for us? *Nothing.* Our kind has splintered and started forming their own gangs, running riot in the streets. They threaten the balance with the humans. Soon, our secret will be out, and we will become the hunted. We need to hunt them. The humans, the witches, the werewolves. We are top of the food chain. *Not them.* We need to take it back."

Nye and Tristan lingered in the shadows, watching the scene unfold before them.

"Diggory," Nye said, recognising the fighter.

"He's arrogant," the knight added beside him. "But his following is gaining momentum fast."

"He couldn't lead his way out of a one-way street."

"That's not the point," Tristan said. "He could unseat you and be in power for a few days before someone else tried their luck. Then we'd be back at square one in an endless loop. Chaos."

Nye's lip curled. A great deal of what the fighter was saying had a lot of truth in it. The vampires of London needed to be brought back into line and fast.

The werewolves never came into the city, and when they did, it wasn't for long. They returned to their forests and abandoned castles before their compulsory change with the moon became a problem.

The witches had always been a part of the city—from its creation a thousand years before and since the Celestines created them. They were never going away.

The only way Nye could see things moving forward with them was by creating an alliance. That was why Gabby was so important, not just because they were friends but because they all wanted the same thing. To continue existing.

But the vampires were the most troublesome of the lot. Natural predators, they were prone to bouts of unprovoked violence. Nye knew this better than anyone.

It was a full-time battle keeping the human world unaware of the thriving supernatural community that lived among them. If all hell broke loose and the fighting spilled onto the streets in broad daylight, it would be bad. *Real bad.*

"I need to send them a message," he said, keeping his voice low so only Tristan could hear.

The knight nodded. "What do you have in mind?"

Nye's lip curled as a devious thought came to mind. He watched the way the vampires crowded around the cage, howling for blood and filling their veins with alcohol to stop their own blood lust from rising too far. They had come here for a spectacle, so he would give them exactly what they wanted. It was the only decent thing to do, after all.

"How are we going to take them on?" a different male vampire asked.

"We need to show them who has the most power," Diggory replied. "We need to lead ourselves out of the darkness and into the light in a shower of blood. We will rip them apart if we have to, but they will obey in the end."

"That's a fine proposal," Nye declared, stepping out of the shadows.

The crowd fell into an abrupt and shocked silence, and a few voices murmured softly in the background as all eyes focused on their leader's impromptu appearance.

"Who do you suggest leads this rebellion?" he went on when Diggory didn't bite. "You?" He looked the fighter up and down and sneered.

"What happened to you, Nye?" Diggory asked. "You were the one-time leader of the Six, feared and respected...and what are you now? *A witch lover*."

Nye didn't react even though Diggory's words had a grain of truth to them. Before Regulus had recruited him, he *had* loved a witch. *Eleanor*.

"I can see you have a rather large axe to grind," Nye said. "So let's fight."

"You want to fight me?" Diggory's eyes widened slightly, giving away his fear even though his voice remained steady.

"Yes," Nye said. "Or are you all bark and no *bite?*"

Diggory snarled and shoved the bottle of beer in his hand at the man standing next to him. "Fine. We'll fight. To the death."

The vampires who had crowded around watching the scene unfold, began to talk heatedly among each other. A fight to the death? Nye didn't expect anything less from a bottom dweller who thought he had the chops to take the crown for his own. It was exactly what he wanted the fighter to do. When he ripped Diggory's head off and made his royal decree, it would send a message that would never be forgotten.

"*Now*," he commanded, his eyes beginning to swirl to black at the promise of blood.

Shucking off his overcoat, he handed it to Tristan as Diggory moved toward the cage in the centre of the warehouse followed by his hangers-on.

"This was exactly what you wanted, wasn't it?" the knight asked.

"Let him think he can take the city from me," Nye replied. "Let him think he has a chance in this moment. When I take his head, the rest will fall in line. Fear and violence, Tristan. It's the only thing they listen to."

"You've got guts."

Nye winked as he began walking away and held his hands open wide. "Consider this my coronation."

Standing in the middle of the cage, he ignored the catcalls from the assembled vampires and began unbuttoning his shirt. Diggory watched him intently, his chest heaving. Nye didn't need to play up to the theatrics of this place by pacing and growling like an animal. What he was about to do would be spectacle enough.

Casting the material aside, his boots followed, and the two vampires faced off.

"I'll enjoy this," Diggory said, his eyes black as he allowed his fangs to grow in. What was Nye thinking about theatrics earlier?

"No more talking, Diggory," he said. "Not unless you're spoken to."

His barb hit home, and Diggory snarled. The fighter lashed out, his fist sailing through the air...right toward Nye's face.

As he dodged the blow, Nye wondered if he should've asked Tristan if he knew the fighter's age. He was four hundred and twenty-one himself, which made him quite formidable paired with his long years of servitude. Just as a fine wine aged over time, so did a vampire's strength. It was too late to contemplate these things about his opponent now.

Ignoring the catcalls from the crowd, he shoved his shoulder into Diggory's gut, using the momentum to lift the vampire from the ground and hurl him backward. The entire cage rattled as his body collided with the chain-link, and before he had a chance to recover, Nye was on him, striking his face with a well-aimed punch.

Blood erupted from Diggory's nose, and he howled with rage, struggling against the hold Nye had on him.

"C'mon, Dig," he taunted. "You're making this too easy. I thought you were meant to be a prize fighter?"

Standing, Nye urged him to get up off his ass and have another shot.

Flying forward, Diggory attacked aggressively,

punching and kicking with as much grace as a pile of shit. Nye moved around each attempt with ease, landing a blow in return for each missed attempt. The sound of Diggory's ribs cracking under the weight of his fists was like music to his ears.

Making a last ditch attempt, Diggory punched with his right and then came back quickly with his left as Nye dodged. Seeing the trap the fighter had made for him, he ducked, the fist meant for his eye sailing right over his head.

Nye had given the fighter a chance to land a punch or two and had remained untouched. There was no way in hell this guy could lead the London underworld. No way in hell. Truthfully, Nye was disappointed with the lack of challenge tonight had presented. Diggory was all talk and no spine.

His patience had run thin, and Nye knew he'd drawn this out long enough. Time to put an end to the fighter's miserable little existence and make him the example he needed him to be.

Launching himself onto the fighter, he sank his fangs into his neck and tore into his flesh like it was butter. Diggory stumbled and fell to his knees with an agonised wail, but still, Nye didn't let go. Fisting his right hand into the vampire's hair and shoving his shoulder with his left, Nye tore with all his strength.

Flesh and bone ripped apart, blood splattering across the concrete floor and coating the vampires who stood closest to the side of the cage as Diggory's head detached from his body.

Pushing to his feet, Nye felt the vampire's blood run from his lips and down his chest, hot and sticky, the scent rancid with the hatred the fighter had felt toward him. Raising his hand, he thrust the severed head into the air.

"*I am your king!*" he roared at the crowd, his fangs throbbing. "If any of you miscreants want to challenge me, *now is your chance.*"

The silence was deafening as he turned around, his gaze burning into every single vampire that was assembled. They stared at him with unmasked fear, not a single soul game enough to step forward and claim the crown.

"This is my city now," he proclaimed, holding up Diggory's head. "You can live in it under my rule, or you can die alone in it. *The choice is yours.*"

Nobody uttered a word. Not after he'd ripped apart his challenger like he was made from soft butter.

Nye's lip curled in satisfaction, and he let Diggory's head fall to the floor. The lump of flesh and bone collided with the concrete, a dull thud echoing through the room.

Long live the king.

CHAPTER 3

Nye's favourite place in the mansion had fast become the study.

Regulus had spent a lot of his time here, surrounded by his vast collection of grimoires and ancient tomes that now belonged to Gabby. The fireplace gave it that homely feeling Nye had missed over the years as the world modernised around him. It reminded him of the grand rooms he'd seen in houses across the country when he was working as a spy under Queen Elizabeth I. That was a long time ago and another life.

Flipping through the dossiers Tristan had compiled on the most notorious vampires in the city, he began narrowing down his choices. He knew all the faces present, but if he was to trust any of them, they had to dig deeper into their comings and goings.

After the other night's spectacle, the underworld was beginning to fall into line and not a moment too soon, but if Nye was going to rule long-term, he needed his own version of the Six, and he needed it soon.

He'd gotten halfway through the pile of folders when the doorbell rang. Rising to his feet, he listened to the still air. Tristan was out, and Gabby was away, so that left him to answer the door himself. As he moved from the study and down the stairs, he made a mental note to compel himself a housekeeper. A pretty one if he could manage it.

Placing his hand on the doorknob, he cast his hearing out and listened to the heartbeat on the other side of the door. It was slightly faster than average, and it put him on edge. Peering through the peephole, he caught sight of a shock of red hair, and he caught a familiar scent.

What was she doing here?

Opening the door, his gaze collided with hers, and she gasped. "Nye."

"Isobel..." He breathed deeply, her sweet scent washing over him, and he tightened his grip on the door. Incredible.

She stared at him, her hazel eyes connecting with his deep brown irises, and neither of them moved. Locked in a silent battle of wills, Nye allowed her to gather her thoughts lest he scare her away.

"I was looking for Alex," she finally said.

"He's not here."

"Oh..."

"He's gone to America with Gabby," he explained. "He didn't tell you?"

She frowned, her forehead creasing. "No. No, he didn't. He hasn't been around since... Well, you know. All that stuff with Aed."

At the mention of the fae hybrid's name, Nye stepped back and gestured for her to come into the house. She didn't hesitate and moved past him, giving away the fact she trusted too easily. Her scent slammed into him like a sledgehammer to the face, and he held his breath. Giving the yard and the street beyond one last glance, he was satisfied no one else was there and closed the door behind her.

No one was lingering, but that didn't mean much. Not in his world. There was no telling who had eyes on the house given his new position and the show of power he'd put on at the fight the other night.

"I didn't mean to intrude," Isobel said softly, sounding distracted. Her gaze flickered around the foyer, her eyes widening as she beheld the size of the house. "I was worried about Alex."

"He's got a lot to worry about himself," Nye replied, watching her closely. "He's a new vampire. These things don't take weeks—it can take years for a vampire to become accustomed to... Time becomes..."

"Irrelevant?"

"Something like that."

She snorted. "I'm sure I'll never be able to grasp the concept of forever."

"He'll be fine," he murmured. "He has Gabby."

"I'm his big sister, Nye. I can't just forget that. He'll always worry me, no matter what he has become."

Nye didn't care about Alex and his transition. Up until five minutes ago, he was more worried about being staked in the back. Now he was concerned about Isobel.

By just showing up, she'd unknowingly made herself known to the London underworld and had put herself in a great amount of danger. It wasn't her fault, she didn't understand, but Nye couldn't let anything happen to her. Her brother was the only founding vampire in the world, and now that Gabby had destroyed the spell that created him, the only one to ever walk it again. That made Alex dangerous, and if something happened to his human sister while she was in Nye's care... He didn't want to think about the mess that would be left of him if he failed.

Isobel mustn't leave the house. Not if he wanted to keep his head and his throne and especially not if Isobel wanted to go on living.

"I need to make a phone call," he said, making Isobel's gaze return to his. "Will you wait?"

A smile appeared on her lips, and he began to feel bad for what he was about to do.

"Sure," she replied.

Returning her smile, he guided her to the sitting room where she sat on the couch, her shoulders stiff with tension. She was worried about being left alone, but she'd be safe inside the mansion. Gabby had made sure of that weeks ago when the deed was signed over into her name. No vampires who were not invited by the witch herself could come inside. Moving upstairs, Nye made sure he was closed inside the study before he pulled out his phone.

Isobel was human and had no way of overhearing his conversation, but he'd been around vampires for far too long. He didn't know how to act around a mortal, and his one memory of what came before was dull at best. Time eroded a great deal of happenings from his mind...nothing remained but the most powerful images—his mother, the battle on board the Spanish galleon that had resulted in the scar marking his face, his death in the lowest reaches of the Tower of London, and then his subsequent transition into a vampire. Those were the things that lingered from his human life.

Putting the past out of his mind, Nye unlocked the screen on his phone and scrolled through the contacts. Pushing the number labeled Sabine, he wondered how much this was going to cost him.

Asking a witch for a favour never came cheap.

Isobel sat awkwardly on the plush leather couch, her gaze taking in every inch of the extravagant sitting room.

This was Gabby's house now? Wow.

She knew Nye lived here with Gabby, but so did Tristan. Nye was the last person she'd expected to answer the door, and in all honesty, she was surprised he was here at all. Gabby was the one she'd imagined seeing when she arrived. She didn't know the first thing about vampires and their sleeping habits but assumed daylight was off limits even with the fancy magic that kept the sun from burning them to a crisp.

And Alex! He'd gone back home without so much as a word. She knew he didn't want to worry her, but she couldn't help it. Her brother was now the most powerful vampire in the world, not to mention immortal and bloodthirsty. *Her little brother!*

His human life would become a liability soon enough when people realised he wasn't ageing, and she knew that was why he'd gone home with Gabby. She just wished he'd told her so she could be there for him. She'd never understand, but she could listen, right?

"Apologies," Nye said from behind her.

Isobel jumped, her heart beating double time. "*Shit.*"

His lips curved into a smile. "I keep forgetting myself," he said. "I don't spend much time with humans."

She was about to say 'only when you eat them', but she closed her mouth. She wasn't sure if she could joke with the vampire anymore.

He was the same man she'd taken a shine to back in Oxford, but something had changed in him. He had the same features, the same stature, and the same scar running across his face, but he was different. He seemed a great deal more serious, but she supposed it was because he was now the head honcho around these parts. At least, that's what Gabby had told her he intended to do after they all parted ways weeks ago.

Anyway, since when did he start talking in such a fancy manner? Saying things like *cannot*, and *apologies*, and not shortening his words at all. He was like a proper English gentleman. He'd only been around a few days, but she missed the roguish vampire who flirted like a total floozy with her. Where had that guy gone?

"I think you should stay here until Alex returns," he said, breaking through her thought pattern.

"What?" She tilted her head to the side, not understanding. "Why? I have to get back to Oxford by Monday. I've got class…"

"I think it would be in your best interests. At least in the short-term."

"Education is in my best interests," she declared. "Besides, Alex could be more than a few days if he's gone home." Home to tie up his human life. It was a sobering thought when she put it that way.

"I don't think you understand my meaning," he came back with. "*I think you should stay here until Alex returns.*"

"Thank you, Nye, but I don't think I can." She didn't add the part where she didn't think it was a good idea to stay in a house with only a four-hundred-year-old vampire and his one-thousand-year-old BFF for company. No matter how easy on the eye they were.

Nye shrugged but didn't try to sway her. He just stood there watching with his creepy unblinking eyes. Turning, she crossed the sitting room and the foyer. Opening the front door, she went to walk through it and smacked face first into an invisible wall. She rubbed her nose and tried again but was met with the same resistance.

"What the hell?" she exclaimed and bashed her fist into the invisible barrier. There was nothing there, but something was stopping her from leaving. *Magic.*

"As I've been trying to say in the most polite way I can," Nye said from behind her, "I cannot let you leave."

Isobel spun on her heel and strode toward the vampire. When she was in reaching distance, she raised her hand and slapped him. Her palm connected with his cheek with a sharp crack, but he didn't even blink.

"How dare you," she said, seething. "You're forcing me to stay? Am I your prisoner now? All I wanted was to see my brother."

"Do you want to die?" he asked, not reacting in the slightest to her anger. "Because that's what you face by going out there. They know you know about us."

"I just got here!"

"That's all it takes," he said firmly. "The house is watched."

"But I'm just a human," she exclaimed, not understanding a single thing about the world she'd been pushed into. "I'm worthless!"

"On the contrary. You're the human sister of the only founding vampire in existence. You show up on my doorstep in broad daylight, and there is only one conclusion they can draw from that. You're now in my care whether you like it or not. I have many enemies who will use you against me. Who better to unseat me than Alex?"

"Alex? The leader of the London underworld?" she scoffed. Alex couldn't lead himself out of a corn maze when they were kids, let alone rule a pack of bloodsucking—

"No," Nye said. "They can't get to me, but he can."

"Manipulate my brother into becoming an assassin?" She crossed her arms over her chest. "You lot are raving mad. All I wanted was to see my brother. He's not here, and now I want to go home. I have class and—"

"I'm sorry, Isobel," he interrupted.

"No, you're not!"

"You're angry now, but you'll understand soon enough." He raised his hand, gesturing for her to follow him.

"It's kidnapping," she cried, following him through

the foyer and up the stairs. "I'm being held against my will."

"And will you call the police?" he asked, unsuccessfully stifling his amusement.

"Fat lot of use that will do."

"So you hope by annoying me enough I'll eventually end up throwing you out?" Opening a door at the end of the hall, he smirked at her.

"A girl can hope." She rolled her eyes and stepped into the room she supposed would be her prison cell for the foreseeable future. Or at least until she could find a way through the magical barrier.

Stopping just inside, her mouth dropped open as she beheld the bedroom Nye had led her into.

The king-sized bed was made up with silver and white silk sheets, a thousand pillows littered along the leather bedhead, and a plush cream-coloured rug underneath. Windows opened out onto the back garden, letting in lots of natural light. A walk-in wardrobe sat beyond, taunting her with floor-to-ceiling mirrors. Bookshelves that were packed full of books, lined another wall while the opposite end of the room was set up as a little sitting area with a couch, armchair, coffee table, rug, and faux fireplace. Above it all was a sleek flat-screen television.

It even had its own private bathroom beyond the walk-in wardrobe. She could see the black marble tiles through the open door and the massive ivory claw-footed bathtub that probably dominated the space.

It was posh. *Very posh.* Just how big was this house?

"This is yours to do with as you wish," Nye said, smiling at her stunned reaction. "I'll send someone to get your things."

"They won't be able to get in," she said, assuming he'd send a vampire lackey to do his bidding.

Nye smiled and shook his head. "You've a lot to learn about us, Isobel."

She threw her hands into the air in defeat. "Well, I guess I've got all the bloody time in the world now. What time does Vampire 101 start?"

His smile turned into a grin, and she shoved down the urge to slap him again. He was so infuriating! Holding her against her will and dumping her in a palace. Sighing, she supposed she could be worse off. Nye had nothing on Aed. That guy had been stark raving mad. Seriously, he'd believed she was the reincarnation of his lost love.

If there was such a thing as being normal in the supernatural world, she supposed Nye was normal enough. He didn't want to make her into an immortal fairy, after all.

"I have some matters to attend to," he said after a moment. "I'll be in the study. First door at the top of the stairs."

Before she could reply, he was gone. One second he was there, the next, she was alone—just like that. *Damn vampires.*

Glancing around the alien-looking room that was

at least four times the size of her tiny shoebox apartment back in Oxford, she shivered. She could pretend she was at an exclusive spa in the Cotswolds if she focused hard enough.

When she put it like that, it didn't sound bad.

Right?

CHAPTER 4

Nye resumed his work on selecting his new elite team of vampires with one ear on his unexpected human houseguest.

As if he didn't have enough problems to deal with, she had to turn up and spin the whirlwind even faster.

"What is Alex's sister doing in the house?"

Nye glanced up at Tristan and rolled his eyes. He knew there was something he was forgetting to tell the knight. In all honesty, the only thing on his mind was the human asleep down the hall. If he listened hard enough and the house was still, he could hear the soft patter of her heart.

"She turned up this afternoon looking for Alex," he explained. "I couldn't let her leave for her own safety."

"He's not going to like it."

Nye closed the file he was reading and said, "Which is why I had a witch lock her inside."

Tristan raised his eyebrows. "You put up a barrier spell?"

"Don't judge me," he retorted. "You know why I had to."

"She's angrier than a bee in a jar, you know."

Nye snorted. "I've made my decision," he said, picking up a small pile of files. "Bring them here. I want to meet with them tonight."

"Here? Where exactly? They can't be invited in, and Isobel—"

"Don't question my orders," he snapped. "We have an outside patio that is delightful this time of year. I don't know these men other than their reputation, and inside the house is a step too far in the wrong direction. Make it happen, Tristan. I won't ask again."

The knight took the files and nodded. "Yes, sir."

He'd never get used to Tristan of all people calling him that. Once, they'd been at each other's throats, but now... It was odd and probably would be for a long time to come. Vampires forgot a lot of things, but love, rivalry, revenge, hatred...they all stuck around like a bad smell.

When he was finally alone again, he cast out his hearing and listened to the comings and goings of Isobel, who was still in the room he'd given her. He smiled as he heard drawers opening and closing as she explored her new home for the foreseeable future. She was a firecracker. The woman had more spark in her than any other human he'd crossed paths with in the last four hundred and twenty-one years.

When he heard her open a window and curse as she found the spell had blanketed the entire mansion, his smile faded.

She'd understand soon enough.

Isobel sat on the couch in her room, staring at the television.

With a sigh, she flipped through the channels, settling on a rerun of the BBC sci-fi classic *Doctor Who*.

As promised, her luggage had appeared at her door moments earlier, and as she rifled through the contents, she cursed when she couldn't find her laptop or notebooks. She wished she'd had the foresight to request Nye's compelled maid bring along her work. Her thesis wouldn't write itself, and considering she was now housemates with two men who had actually lived through the Tudor dynasty of England, she could've gotten some real insight.

But the real kicker was when she realised Nye had lifted her mobile phone from her purse. No calling her brother for help.

Then there was her other more immediate predicament. *She was starving.*

Where the hell was the kitchen, and more importantly, was there any food in it?

Finally, she couldn't handle it anymore. Wrenching open the door to her room, she marched down the hall, wild with anger.

Opening the door that Nye had said was the study, she peered inside and found it empty. It was yet another room that was grand beyond comprehension. The walls were lined from top to bottom with leather-bound books with a large desk taking up most of the space to one side. On the other wall was a fancy open fireplace crackling merrily with a small orange glow.

Closing the door, she went down the stairs, listening for movement ahead, but she couldn't hear a thing. Was she alone? Had they all gone out stalking dinner without asking her if she was hungry? Had they forgotten humans had to eat food to survive? Not blood but roast meat, vegetables, pasta, chicken, sausages... At the thought of all that deliciousness, her stomach began to rumble.

Downstairs, she found more splendours. Paintings by famous artists that looked like originals hung on the walls—paintings that should be in museums and others that historians thought were lost to the ages— and she gaped at each one. There had to be at least ten million pounds worth of them just in the rooms she'd seen. *Who were these people?*

When she found the kitchen, she threw her hands into the air. *"You've got to be kidding me!"*

The kitchen was *huge*. Stainless steel appliances, marble bench-tops, a giant two-door refrigerator, ovens and sinks, a large island in the middle of it all... It was like she was inside one of those million-dollar home lifestyle shows.

Through the windows, she saw light and movement outside and circled around the bench. Nye was about to get a piece of her mind, and it wasn't the good part.

Standing in the open doorway, she hesitated. Not because she couldn't go outside but because there was a group of strange but dangerous-looking men standing before a serious-looking Nye on the patio. She'd stumbled upon something that was none of her business, and as they all turned their heads toward her, her heart began to beat faster.

The strangers—she counted six—all started looking very...hungry.

Nye turned back to the men without acknowledging her and waved his hand like she was an annoyance.

"Forgive the intrusion. She belongs to me," he said absently.

She went to open her mouth to complain, but another glance at the six mean-looking thugs on the back patio had her zipping her lips closed. She supposed she didn't mind 'belonging' to Nye if it meant his royal subjects would leave her alone.

"Tristan," he said, pointing at her.

Tristan emerged from where he'd been hidden

behind the group and came toward her, his expression impassive.

Suddenly, her bravado felt extremely rash and stupid. She didn't belong in this world, and by stumbling into what looked like a business meeting, she'd made that painfully obvious. She was a silly little lamb waiting for the trip to the slaughterhouse.

"I'm sorry," she said as Tristan guided her through the kitchen and away from whatever was going on outside. "I was hungry, and I wasn't sure... I didn't know if you kept food or if I was supposed to ask..."

"He should have told you he was meetin' them," Tristan said kindly. "They can't come inside, just as you can't go out."

"Oh..." Her stomach growled again, and she shuffled from foot to foot.

"I can have something delivered for you," he went on, his gaze dropping to her stomach. The rumble had sounded loud to her, and she wondered if it was like a clap of thunder to his sensitive ears. "What do you like?"

Isobel shrugged. "I don't know. Pizza? That's easy enough, I suppose..."

Tristan smiled. "I'll arrange it." Before he moved off, he hesitated. "Are you feelin' well?"

"Annoyed mostly." Isobel frowned and glanced back toward the garden. "He sounds like..."

"Regulus," the knight finished for her.

"Gabby's Regulus?" She'd never met the Roman

but had heard plenty of stories. The bad guy with a soft spot for her friend.

"Yes. Nye is using what he knows the vampires will respond to. Regulus had a particular flair, after all."

"If that flair extends to me belonging to him, he can just flair off."

Tristan chuckled. "It's in your best interests that he claims you. They need to think you're nothin' but his human plaything. You can probably understand why."

"Alex," she said, rolling her eyes.

"You're precious to him and that warrants protecting."

Precious to Alex...or Nye? Her fragile human heart wanted to say both, but she knew Nye was looking out for himself by keeping her here. He'd made it clear all he worried about was his precious crown, and she'd only been incarcerated a few hours. She wasn't a stupid little girl with a crush. She was working on her Masters degree at Oxford University. No one could get that far without developing an analytical brain in their head.

"Wait in your room," Tristan said, watching her shifting features closely. "I'll bring the food to you when it arrives."

As he turned, she wondered if it was too much to ask if they could get her laptop. Deciding there was no harm, she said, "Can I ask for something?"

The knight stopped and nodded. "Of course."

"Someone brought me my clothes, but if I'm going to be here for a while... My thesis..." She swallowed, feeling like a fish out of water. "Can someone bring my laptop and notebooks?"

His lips curved into a smile, and he nodded.

"Thank you..."

"If you need anythin' else, let me know."

Then he just disappeared in a whoosh of air, leaving her skin tingling. Bloody vampires!

Climbing the stairs, she was glad Tristan had been so nice to her, but she still felt uneasy...and unwanted.

She'd had her life all figured out, from her studies and career to all the places she wanted to travel and projects she wanted to work on before settling into a cushy position as a curator at one of the big archaeological museums. And now?

Now that she knew the things she did about the world, she wasn't sure she belonged anywhere.

The morning arrived, and Isobel still felt uneasy.

Her annoyance was rising, turning into a full-blown case of pissed off. It seemed all good and well spending one night in forced imprisonment, but in the cold, hard light of the next day, it wasn't fun anymore. She'd pretended, but it was a flimsy excuse for Nye's shitty behaviour.

Locking her in here against her will with magic!

Deciding to make herself at home, she took the last of the pizza downstairs and found the kitchen. It looked big in the sunshine, the large windows letting in all the natural light bathing the garden outside. Staring across the greenery as she dumped the old food into the bin, she marvelled at the olive tree. She never knew they could grow like that in London due to the weather... Shaking her head, she knew it was probably because of magic. Everything around here was.

Deciding breakfast was a good option, she walked over to the fridge and said a silent prayer. *Please have something edible in there.*

Opening the door, she gasped when she set eyes on the contents. It was full of clear, heavy-duty, hospital grade bags of blood. Screwing up her face in disgust, she grabbed the pint of milk on the door and slammed the fridge closed.

Ugh, *vampires*. She should've known.

Rummaging through all the cupboards, she found enough ingredients to make some basic pancakes. She'd have to have them with butter, but it was better than pizza that had turned to cardboard.

Digging in her pocket, she plugged her MP3 player into the speakers sitting on the bench-top, selected her favourite playlist, and hit play with flourish. She hoped Nye was home so she could annoy the crap out of him with the most obnoxious, loud rock music she could find. How dare he keep her locked in here against her will? It wasn't the worst place to be held prisoner, but considering she was stuck with a bunch of vampires, it kinda sucked. Pun intended.

Tearing around the kitchen, she made herself at home like she'd been instructed, whipping up batter and heating a frying pan on the oversized stove. She twirled and danced as she flipped the pancakes, cooking them until they were golden on both sides and all the batter had disappeared. Better to make some supplies incase these vampires forgot her again.

As she turned around and picked up the plate, her gaze collided with Nye. She cried out, sliding the plate onto the bench before she dropped the lot on the floor, and clutched her chest.

"*Nye!*" she screeched at him. "Don't do that."

A lazy grin spread across his face. "But I was enjoying the routine."

She glared at him and turned on her heel, switching off the stovetop. "I'm not all super hearing like you, so please keep that in mind unless you want me to die of a heart attack."

He materialised next to her, and she yelped again. "Your wish is my command."

"*Asshole!*"

"I've been called much worse," he said with a shrug.

Isobel picked up the pan and dumped it in the sink, the water hissing as it hit the hot steel. "Oh, I'm sure you have."

"Pancakes?" he asked, ignoring her quip.

"Yeah. You don't have much in the way of food."

He watched as she sidled up to the island and blew on the hot pancakes. She would be lying to herself if she said she had not been attracted to the vampire, but that was when she'd first met him in Oxford. Now he was a major asshole. It was like the power had gone to his head.

"What do you need?" he asked after a moment. "Make a list, and I will make sure you get it."

Isobel rolled her eyes. "That's it?" she asked.

His eyebrows rose.

"Oh, don't give me that look." She dumped a pancake onto a plate and opened the lid on the butter, digging a knife into the spread.

"I'm not sure I get your meaning."

She waved the butter-laden knife at him. "You get my meaning, you four-hundred-year-old smartass."

Nye grinned, leaning against the bench. "You're perceptive."

"You know it's creepy watching me eat, right?"

He laughed, and she hated how handsome he was despite his scar and how much he irritated her.

"You're trying to make me like you, Nye, and I'm not giving in."

"But you already like me," he said with a wink, some of the vampire she'd originally met coming back to the surface.

"Let me go home," she said through a sigh. "I can't imagine how much of a drag it must be having me here all the time. I mean, I walk in on your super secret vampire meetings…" Her cheeks began to heat as his words came back to her. *She belongs to me.*

His expression changed from inviting to…nothing. All emotion ceased to exist. "I cannot let you leave, Isobel. You know that."

"Nye—"

He held up a hand to silence her. "Your life is at stake."

God, she was so puny and weak next to him and her brother. A strong mind wasn't enough in this world. At best, she was a dead weight, nothing but an insignificant human being and utterly defenceless. She hated that he kept reminding her with his refusal to let her go.

She dropped her head and rubbed her eyes, knowing that she wasn't going to convince him anytime soon. "I'll make a list."

She felt him shift as he pushed off the bench and backed away. "I'll make sure someone gets it to you by this evening."

When she finally glanced up, she was alone.

CHAPTER 5

Nye was rather pleased with the men he'd selected to become the new Six. Every king needed to have his elite guard, after all.

Wainwright, Fox, Farmer, Judd, Felixstowe, and Reed—all varying ages from eight hundred to as little as a few decades—were the men who would be able to carry out his orders and see they would completed with enthusiasm. When presented with the opportunity to pick up where Nye's group had left off, all had jumped at the chance.

Tristan had done his research well, and only time and a few missions would tell the real story of where their allegiance lay.

He'd set them up in the original Six's old apartment in Camden, making sure they had everything they needed. It was one of the things that had made his time with the group more comfortable, and if anyone knew how to keep men like these pleased, it was he.

Isobel had almost derailed the meeting at the mansion by turning up right in the middle of it. Six— or was it seven—pairs of hungry eyes had latched onto her, and he'd had to make a bold statement he knew she'd be offended by. Her reaction was clear in the kitchen yesterday morning. Anger, frustration...it was ruling her actions, but it was to be expected.

Nye stood in the foyer of the mansion and breathed deeply. Her scent was everywhere, and it filled his senses to the brim. Seven pairs of hungry eyes, then.

He listened to the sound of her furious tapping on her computer keyboard and cursed to himself. Turning, he opened the front door and disappeared out into the night in case temptation drove him to her bedroom door.

As Nye walked, he allowed his thoughts to drift to the tasks requiring his attention—pinpointing areas of the city that were still on tenterhooks, squashing the gangs of vampires who'd taken up residence in the council flat areas of Brixton, and the witches who'd begun congregating on the outer limits of the city. He'd have to coordinate with the Six to handle some of these threats before the week was out.

Nye had ventured all the way into the heart of London before he realised. He'd automatically stopped at the pedestrian lights at Tottenham Court Road and

Oxford Street with a group of humans waiting to cross. Breathing deeply, he caught the scent of a woman standing to his right. Glancing at her, he saw her shock of red hair, which was almost the same copper as Isobel's, and found himself drawn in her direction.

Sensing his gaze on her, the woman turned, and their eyes met. Her lips began to curve into a smile, but then revulsion flickered across her features as she beheld the jagged scar running across his face. Nye scowled as she hastily turned away. Isobel didn't recoil when she first saw him. She'd stared right at him with a curiosity that had taken his breath away, and she'd asked, 'What happened to your face?'

The lights changed and the woman who was a poor substitute for the real thing moved off with the group of people waiting to cross, and he followed at a distance, thoroughly annoyed at her shallowness. He walked down Charing Cross Road, past theatres and restaurants—all of them packed to the brim with human blood bags and wondered how her blood would taste. Spicy or sweet?

Finally, the woman seemed to reach her destination as she weaved through the throng of people waiting outside the Palace Theatre. The facade was lit up with signs for the musical *The Commitments*, and Nye stopped at the edge of the group, watching the redhead as she greeted her friends.

His phone began to ring in his pocket, the vibration

irritating his skin. Without breaking his gaze away from the woman, he pulled it out and answered.

"What is it?" he asked, allowing the pretty redhead to disappear into the crowd milling around the entrance.

"There's a situation," Tristan replied.

"What kind of situation?"

"Reed called," he said. "They found a desiccated vampire strung up with a strange symbol carved into his chest."

That's when he saw it. The witch's rune scrawled on the side of the theatre in what looked like red paint *or blood*. A perfect circle cut in three diagonal parts with heavy brushstrokes, the centre line finishing off at the bottom with something akin to an asterisk. He knew that image. He'd seen it before...

"Nye?"

Tristan's voice broke through his foggy mind, and he blinked, the image dissolving. The side of the building was blank like nothing was ever there to begin with, and he was left confused as to whether it was witchy mind tricks or his own insecurities playing with him.

"Where?" he asked, turning away from the theatre.

"The construction site on Queen Victoria Street..."

"Cheapside," he mused.

He'd grown up there, in the slums not far from the bustling marketplace of the Middle Ages. Cheapside stood in the shadow of St. Paul's Cathedral and had been full of merchants, rich and poor. Since his mother had been one of them, selling her meagre wares seven days a week so they had enough coin to eat and keep a roof over their heads, Nye had come to know the district like the back of his own hand. He'd been known to pickpocket unsuspecting gentlemen on many occasions. That was the only way they knew to survive in those days.

Now Cheapside was home to a modern shopping centre, One New Change, and various high-end retail stores. Progress didn't slow for any one man.

"I'm not far from there," Nye went on. "I'll meet you at the site."

Hanging up the call, he took one more glance back at the theatre. The wall was still blank, but his blood thrummed in his veins, making him uneasy. It couldn't be a coincidence.

When he arrived at the construction site, he recognised Reed standing with Tristan at the street entrance.

The vampire stood a head taller than both of them, his muscled frame giving the vampire an air of added strength. Being born in the nineteenth century meant that he had been afforded the medical knowledge his elders hadn't. Simply put, humanity had evolved itself into a race of giants compared to the people of the Dark and Middle Ages.

Nye saw a lot of himself in the young vampire, and he'd pegged him to become the official leader of the Six before long. He was ruthless and bloodthirsty but had a calm and collected manner about him. He thought about his decisions, making the most of any given situation. And he was a handsome bastard.

"The security guards have been compelled, sir," Reed said as Nye came to a halt. "The area has been contained. The others have gone to make sure the perimeter is watertight."

"Good. Where is the body?"

"We took him down," Reed said, guiding him forward through the construction site. "He was just hanging there for anyone to see."

"Hanging how?"

"Steel rods were impaled through his wrists and ankles. The ends were in the ground hoisting him up about twenty feet. There was another rod in his spine to keep him from sagging," the vampire explained. "I don't know how they got him up there, but it was sight." They came to a stop beside a tarp that had been laid over the body. "Here he is."

Kneeling beside the corpse, Nye lifted the covering off him and revealed what he came to verify. The vampire was desiccated, his veins bulging from grey flesh and very much dead. His gaze fixed on his bare torso and the symbol he already knew he was going to find.

There was nothing crude about the way the flesh had been sliced. Every stroke was deliberate and well-practiced. The blade used had been sharper than a diamond. The circle was perfect in execution, and each diagonal stroke never wavered.

Staring down at the gashes, he frowned. It was the same symbol he'd seen painted on the side of the theatre, and in that moment, he knew he hadn't been imagining it. If a witch had put this here, then only one coven could be responsible for it. The thought chilled his already dead body to pure ice.

The Unhallowed.

The ancient coven of witches had died out three hundred years before, so why was one of their symbols carved into the chest of one of his vampires? Was it a copycat, or was the coven still around?

"They found the same image painted on walls throughout the city," Tristan said. "It never changes shape or form."

That confirmed what he already knew about the image he'd seen earlier, which hadn't been a hallucination. It was meant for his eyes only.

"It's a warning," Nye said, rising to his feet.

"From who?" the knight mused out loud. "And for what?"

Nye snorted and cast his gaze back to the dead vampire. If it was the Unhallowed, then he had a big problem on his hands. They all did. Keeping the knowledge to himself would cause more problems than not when more bodies began to show. This was the first of many—he didn't have any doubt about that.

"The Unhallowed," he said, turning back to Tristan and Reed.

"The who?" the young vampire asked.

"The Unhallowed were a coven of witches I was led to believe had died out three hundred years ago. By the looks of him, this is no longer the case. It may be a follower of their cult...or it may be a resurgence. Either way, I am not taking any chances."

"A cult?" Tristan asked. "I've never heard of this coven before."

"They deal in dark magic. Blood sacrifices and rituals that call on the deepest parts of the spirit world... They channel living creatures for more power."

"Like vampires," Reed said, glancing uneasily at the corpse.

"No matter who it is, they have to be stopped before they kill again," Nye said, turning away.

"So what do we do now?" the young vampire asked.

Nye didn't know how to stop them short of cutting off their heads. A vivid memory appeared in his mind's eye, and he began to grind his teeth. *Eleanor.* She was an Unhallowed witch who he'd deigned loving until the coven found out. That day in the woods surrounding York...for all he knew the symbol she'd carved into his forehead was the same one that adorned that poor bastard behind him.

"Sir?"

Narrowing his eyes, he turned to face Reed. "Take the body away, and burn it. No evidence is to be left behind, do you understand?"

He glanced at Tristan before asking, "Is that all?"

Allowing his anger to trickle to the surface, Nye felt his skin crawl as his eyes began to change into darkness. "*That is all.*"

Turning, he walked away and disappeared into the darkness, his senses stretching out around him, but nothing supernatural moved apart from the vampires he'd left behind him.

The fact that the symbols had started appearing now was not a coincidence. He was in a position of power, well-known and well-situated in the city. He'd emerged from the shadows, and so had the witches.

Nye'd had a target on his back for a very long time, one he thought he'd been rid of for three hundred years. He'd killed the daughter of the Unhallowed matriarch, and it had sparked the beginning of their demise. If they had returned, then it wouldn't be long before they came for him. Vampires had long memories, but those of a witch ran deep into a place of eternal vengeance.

Long story short, he was screwed.

As he walked, he thought of sweet, innocent Isobel and began to regret the circumstances she now found herself among. It may not be safe enough to let her leave once Alex and Gabby returned. It had only been two days since she'd arrived, and now he had a serial killer on his hands. A serial killer who knew who he was and what he'd done all that time ago... If they thought they could use Isobel to get to him, they would.

Nye was fast learning what it meant to be a ruler in this city.

Nye walked all the way to his old haunt, The Good Mixer.

Pulling up a stool in a dark corner, he gestured for the entire bottle of scotch and added a bottle of whisky for variation. Beer wasn't strong enough to dampen the pooled anger and dread that had settled in his stomach.

He thought over everything he knew about the Unhallowed, but it wasn't a great deal. Even when he'd been gallivanting around York with Eleanor, he hadn't learned much. He'd been a new vampire then and very much at the mercy of his emotions, which had been tangled up in his heart and the love they'd shared in his bed.

When the coven had realised where she'd been spending most of her time, they'd gotten inside her head and turned her against him. The day he'd met her outside of York Minster, she'd lured him to the woods to kill him. No, that wasn't quite right. She'd rendered him immobile and had carved a symbol into his forehead. Why? He never knew, but perhaps she had been going to channel his energy, picking his corpse clean of all the power she could before discarding him to the predators that roamed the wilderness.

"He said it was carved into his chest."

Nye's ears pricked as yet another drunken conversation between vampires became heated behind him. What was it about this place that attracted such imbeciles? It was a vampire haunt, but it wasn't impenetrable to other supernatural creatures...or humans. Unwanted ears still lingered here as much as they did anywhere else in the city, and right now, he couldn't take any chances the Unhallowed were lurking.

"Witches," someone else said. "They're always trying to siphon power. That's what I think the symbol is for. There's no other explanation. I saw one inside the Tube station. It was smeared on the wall in blood, and everyone around me didn't seem to care..."

"Then the humans can't see them," a gruff-sounding man said. "Only us."

"I've seen them, too," another man said. "There was one on the side of the bank just down on the High Street."

"Is it the same one that was on the body?"

"That's what Bronny said," a new voice chimed in. "He saw it and told Reed."

"Reed?" the gruff vampire asked. "He's been made one of the Six, did you know that? He's nothing but a bootlicker."

Nye glanced at the time on his phone and saw that only three hours had passed since he'd left the construction site. Word spread quickly, but he shouldn't be surprised about that considering there were many waiting for him to screw up his duties.

Downing the last of the whisky, he turned around on the stool and rose to his feet. Straightening his shirt and smoothing his jacket into place, he emerged from his dark corner to put a stop to the excessive *and loud* gossiping.

"I don't know why you people keep bad-mouthing me when you know I like to drink here," he said, placing a firm hand on the nearest vampire's shoulder. "You're acting like a group of gossiping high school mean girls, and nobody likes a *bitch*."

The group fell silent, their eyes widening as they realised their king stood among them. It reminded him of the last time he was here...which was only last week. Apparently, winning a fight by tearing apart his opponent with his bare hands was not enough for some people.

"You've got nothing much to say now, do you?" he went on as they stared at him, each and every one of them squirming in their seats.

No one replied, the silence stretching to the rest of the pub.

Fisting his hands into the vampire's shirt, Nye dragged him from his seat and wrenched him close. "Let it be known that any vampire who brings me the head of the witch responsible will be rewarded beyond compare. No one threatens my people and lives to boast about it, do you understand?" The vampire stared at him, fear rendering him speechless. "*Do you understand?*"

Finally, the man nodded, and Nye let him go. Smoothing down his shirt and buttoning his suit jacket, he looked over the group of vampires and those around them who had stopped their drinking to stare.

"This brazen attack by these witches on one of our own is a personal attack on me," he declared. "*Blood will be repaid in blood*, but I will not tolerate insubordination. We are on the brink of war with these witches..." He turned around, looking at every man and woman in the rear of the pub. "A war I do not want to have and a war that I want to end swiftly. Bring me their heads, and you'll see how generous your new king really is."

Picking up the half-finished bottle of scotch, he moved through the room. As he stepped outside into the night, sound erupted from within the pub, voices chattering earnestly, all of them talking about Nye and his offer.

He had a kingdom at his disposal and a witch problem that would never go away until he struck with everything he had. Why not use the hundreds of

London vampires to his advantage? A swift end to a brewing war. With any luck, there'd be a severed head or two on his desk by the end of the week, and the Unhallowed would be dead once more.

It was a fine plan.

CHAPTER 6

When Nye returned to the mansion, Tristan was waiting for him in the study.

"Did Reed dispose of the corpse?" he asked, sitting by the fireplace.

"He sent confirmation through an hour ago," the knight replied, sitting across from him.

The night had worn into the small hours of the morning, and as Nye listened to the sounds inside the mansion, he heard the soft patter of Isobel's heartbeat three rooms down. Of all the opportune times for her to show up, she had to come at the worst one.

"Do you want to tell me about the Unhallowed and how you know so much about them?" Tristan asked, pulling his attention back to the matter at hand.

"Does it matter how?" he asked, the two bottles of alcohol he'd consumed still not quite enough to calm the inner beast.

"Yes, it does. The symbols are spreadin' at an

alarmin' rate," Tristan said, handing Nye his phone, which had a whole reel of photographs. "Vampires all over the city have been sendin' them to the Six, who have sent them to me."

Nye swiped through the images, the symbol burning into his long-term memory. It had only been nine hours since he stood outside that theatre and saw the symbol for the first time. It was like a disease, multiplying and spreading like a cancer, attacking from every side...even from within.

Vampires were already talking about the defiled corpse. They were seeing witches runes painted in blood that only supernatural eyes could behold and were still questioning their king's ability to deal with such a problem. *Nine hours.* For creatures who weren't shackled to a little thing called time, they sure worked fast.

"Have there been any more bodies?" he asked.

"No, but I'm suspectin' it'll only be a matter of time. Somethin' about this smells like a long time in the makin'."

About four hundred years, Nye thought. Witches loved to hold a grudge when someone cuts off the head of one of their own.

"Tell me about the Unhallowed," the knight commanded.

Nye snorted, tossing the phone onto the table beside him.

"*Nye.* You've encountered them before. If we're

goin' to put an end to this before it gets any worse, we need to know everythin'."

"We? You and me?" Nye pointed between them and rolled his eyes.

"Of course. We hated one another for a long time, but after everythin' that happened with Aed... I made you a promise by stayin' behind to help. This is me helpin'."

Miracles never ceased...

"Yes, I've encountered them before. *Intimately*," Nye said after a moment of silent staring at the knight. "It was a long time ago, about ten years or so after I was turned—1603..."

"You said you had intimate knowledge..."

"Her name was Eleanor," Nye said, staring into the fireplace.

"You fell in love with one of them?" the knight asked, his eyebrows rising.

"What a conclusion to jump to."

"It's obviously the right one."

"I was lost for a long time, and she provided meaning."

"But she was one of the Unhallowed?"

Nye nodded. "Eleanor was the daughter of the Unhallowed's matriarch, their leader as chosen by the darkest spirits of the ether. They were unaware of what her daughter was doing in her spare time, and when they inevitably found out, they poisoned Eleanor's mind against me." As he spoke, he could almost feel the snow against his skin as he lay immobile, her knife slicing through his flesh, the tip grinding against his skull. "She lured me out into the woods...I would've gone anywhere with her back then, so I followed. It was there that she turned on me, using her magic to... I didn't understand at the time, but she was going to siphon my energy in the same way as that corpse..."

"She obviously failed," Tristan said, his voice devoid of emotion. He was keeping himself impassive —as an advisor should. "How?"

"Not in any way that's useful for our current situation," Nye went on. "The day I was attacked by Eleanor was also the day I first became aware of Regulus. He was the one who stopped her. He saved me from her magic, and I was able to kill her on the spot."

"And that's how you came to be part of the Six. Through obligation." It was a statement and a truer one if ever he heard it.

"In return, Regulus helped put an end to the Unhallowed's relentless hunting of me. They wanted revenge, but it was denied. Two generations of those witches pursued me until they became no more."

"If this isn't a copycat and they're back, then you're in danger," Tristan said.

"Yes, it would appear so, but this time, it's different. I have an entire city out looking for them. They will be found before long, and they will be ended once more."

Tristan's brow creased, and he began to look

displeased. Nye knew the vampire had a great deal he was holding back on, and usually, his opinion was righteous at best. Tristan had the highest horse of them all, but it was the way he was brought up and the way he'd defined his life as a vampire in the wake of the horrors he'd witnessed as a Knights Templar of the Crusades. His whole chivalry act still pissed Nye off, no matter the reason for it.

"Hell, Tristan," he cursed. "If you have something to say, just bloody say it. It irritates me no end when you sit there looking like you've been sucking on a lemon."

"Regulus wouldn't have allowed any vampire to be slaughtered by a witch," the knight said. "Your hold over the London vampires is hangin' by a thread. You have to keep them in line and not drag them into a four-hundred-year-old personal revenge plot."

Nye's eyes narrowed in warning. "Don't you think I know that? This needs to end swiftly, and they can make that happen. I can't canvass the entire city alone before the next body appears."

"And if they find out you're harborin' a human woman, they won't be happy."

"The Six won't talk," he snapped. "Isobel is here for a very good reason, and you know it. Now more so than ever. The Unhallowed will use her against me if they find out she means..." He closed his mouth and tightened his grip around the arm of the chair. "No matter what happens, she'll be hurt, and I'd rather it be by my hand in this house where she can keep her life."

Tristan eyed him, and if he thought Nye's concern over Isobel was more than it should be, he didn't mention it. "Well, you had better deliver on your promises. Otherwise, the entire London vampire community will be at your door clamorin' for your head."

"Get out," Nye snapped, thoroughly annoyed at the knight's barrage of home truths.

Tristan rose to his feet, inclined his head, and retreated out of the study, leaving Nye to his own devices.

He sank back into the armchair and stared at the dying flames in the fireplace, his mind swirling with the weight of his predicament.

Regulus spent his entire vampire life hunting and destroying the Tuatha hybrids, and not once had he delegated the task to another. What did that say about his successor if he sent the whole city after his own problems? Not much and he'd already done just that... but there was the fact that Nye and the original Six had spent a great deal of time hunting Aya, the Celestine hybrid, for him, too. Was this any different? The Unhallowed had declared open war against all vampire kind as far as he was concerned. Perhaps he had made the right call.

Nye couldn't shake the feeling he'd just failed his first real challenge as leader of the London vampires.

Only time would tell if things would come crashing down.

Isobel stood in the foyer of the mansion, feeling like she was the last human being on earth.

The house had been a hive of activity the last two nights, and she had no idea what everyone was so worked up about—not that they'd tell her, anyway. Since the incident at breakfast the other morning, she'd seen Nye a total of zero times.

Apart from Tristan checking in on her yesterday afternoon, she may as well be in solitary confinement.

Annoyed at feeling like she was confined to the bedroom, she decided she'd go out and see the world, meaning she wanted to inspect the treasure trove of art that hung all over the walls.

The one that had caught her eye was before her, the canvas mounted in a golden frame with a hand-painted nameplate at the bottom. It didn't bear the artist's name, but it had the title of the work, *The Dream of Human Life*. History said the artist, Michelangelo, had only drawn the image by hand. A sketch on paper was all that future generations had. He'd never actually painted it...only his followers after his death had committed the image to colour.

Staring intently at the brushstrokes and studying the application of gold leaf, she was sure of it. It was a

Michelangelo. *An original.* He'd painted the entire ceiling of the Sistine Chapel in Rome, which included the famous image of *The Creation of David.* He'd sculpted one of the most iconic marble statues in human history, *David*, and here was a piece painted by the master's own hand, a painting history said had never been created, hanging in a vampire's house in Hampstead, London. It was criminal.

"Don't they know what this is?" she whispered, completely aghast. If it went up for auction, she was sure it'd fetch upwards of ten million pounds. Just for this one! When Gabby got back, she'd have to tell her how rich she really was.

A thump from outside pulled her attention and she turned, staring at the giant door that taunted her with its inability to grant her freedom.

When no other sound followed, no knocking or doorbell ringing, she hesitated. She waited a moment, silently debating on whether she should open the door or not.

Tristan said no vampires could come inside unless invited by Gabby. If she couldn't get out, did that mean the house was impenetrable to other humans, too? She didn't know if it extended to witches and other creatures as well or if it was just vampires. *Wait,* how many other supernatural creatures were out there? Aed was one of the Tuatha fae, so fairies were a thing, an extinct thing, but they were real at some point. Werewolves? Were *they* a thing?

She'd been walking around her whole life among these creatures blissfully unaware and totally safe, so what was different now that she knew? Nothing. It was the uncertainty in her own mind stopping her.

Deciding she'd take the risk, Isobel stepped forward and took charge.

Opening the front door, she found a dagger embedded into the wood. A piece of parchment was stuck beneath it, like the knife was some kind of over-the-top drawing pin. What the hell? That explained the thud.

Swinging the door further inside, Isobel narrowed her eyes when she realised the paper was blank. It made no sense. Who would knife the door with a blank note? These people were bloody crazy.

Raising her hand, she went to stroke the paper, wondering if touch would reveal anything.

"Don't touch that."

Her gaze collided with Nye's as she turned, her fingers still poised in the air. Her heart did a flip in her chest and she flinched, knowing he heard everything. No being covert about stupid, unobtainable crushes in this house. At least this one she could pass off as being startled.

"What is it?" she asked.

He moved forward fluidly and opened the door as far as it would go. Staring at the dagger and the note, he frowned but didn't reveal a single one of this thoughts.

"Nye?"

He glanced at Isobel. "It's none of your concern. Go back inside."

"I am inside," she said, bashing her fist against the invisible barrier, the sunshine and twittering birds taunting her from beyond. "I'm so inside it's painful."

He grasped the hilt of the dagger and pulled, his free hand plucking away the parchment before it fluttered to the ground.

"It's blank," she said. "Is it supposed to mean something?"

"It's not blank," Nye murmured. "Only supernatural creatures can see..."

"Well, glad we cleared up how plain boring I am."

Nye seemed to stiffen, his entire body freezing like he was a sculpture in a museum. Then he shut the front door, the wood driving home with a bang, and closed out the world beyond.

"You are not plain boring," he said, ignoring the moment when she jumped out of her skin at the abrupt slam of the door.

"I'm clueless, though," she retorted, letting the fear she'd been carrying around since she got here fall away—the fear of being an inconvenience, the fear of being lunch, and the fear of being a useless human being. She just let it go and let the real Isobel shine. "I have no idea what to do or what is going on around this place. I'm stuck here for God knows how long, and I can't help. I rely on Tristan to bring me food for heaven's sake! I'm not strong or fast… I'm not supernatural…" She gestured to the paper he held in his hand. "I'm just a plain human being with nothing—"

"You're human, Isobel," he interrupted. "*Human.*"

She rolled her eyes. "*Right.* Like that's the answer to everything."

Nye seemed to creep closer, his expression darkening like thunder. "You don't know how many of us wish we could go back. How many of us were forced into this life…" His lip curled. "*You don't know.*"

She sucked in a sharp breath, her eyes widening. "You were forced to become…"

"Go upstairs," he commanded.

"*No.*" She almost stamped her foot to punctuate her sentence.

"Isobel…"

"Do you know what that is?" she asked, pointing to the Michelangelo.

"It's a painting," he replied, his stature seeming to relax.

"It's a Michelangelo," she declared. "An *unknown* Michelangelo. It's worth at least ten million pounds."

He tilted his head to the side. "What's that got to do with anything?"

Isobel didn't know. She didn't know anything. Her life was spiralling out of control, and the only thing she could grasp was history. History, antiquity, and art. The mansion was full to the brim with it, and it was the only thing she understood.

"This I know," she said, jabbing a finger at the painting.

"I see..." Nye mused.

"And that one behind you, I'm pretty sure it's an early version of Raphael's *The Three Graces*." The image of three naked women was iconic for its time. The Renaissance was famous for its numerous depictions of a fuller-figured woman, and this one was on the slimmer side but not to the point of the modern ideal of beauty. *The Three Graces* were goddesses of charm, beauty, and creativity. It was a stunning image even though it appeared to be a study for the final product.

"The ass painting?" the vampire asked, his lip quirking.

"The ass..." She threw her hands into the air. "I don't understand you."

"That makes two of us," he quipped. "You like the ass painting."

"You're saying that on purpose."

"It took your mind off the puny human shame spiral you were riding, didn't it?"

And just like that, the vampire she'd met back in Oxford was at the surface, the pompous king of the London underworld shoved aside in favour of some harmless flirting. Was it harmless, though? The shame spiral was fast turning into a merry-go-round of another kind.

"What's the notepaper for?" she asked, nodding to the dagger and parchment he still clutched.

"It's vampire business," he replied, his smile fading. "Don't feel the need to concern yourself with it, Isobel."

"Seems like nasty vampire business, then," she spat. "Haven't they heard of Royal Mail? Learn to lick a stamp."

Nye's eyebrows rose, but she knew she was only making herself suffer if she stuck around to argue. He'd never tell her what was going on, let alone allow her to help. So she turned on her heel and stormed away, stomping up the stairs in a whirlwind of utter annoyance.

He'd implied her humanity was precious, that he'd do anything to have the choice...but right now, she couldn't see any advantage in it at all. She was an outsider and was constantly reminded of it like it was a failing rather than a treasure to be coveted.

Bloody vampires. She just wanted to go home and forget this ever happened. She wanted to go back to how things used to be.

Hurry up, Alex.

Closing the door to the study behind him, Nye placed the note and dagger on the desk.

His head was full of Isobel, and her frustration had begun to rub off on him even though their encounter had lasted all of five minutes. That was how much the human woman had crawled under his cold, dead skin despite his attempts to keep her at arm's length.

Her talk of the paintings downstairs... She was intelligent and knowledgeable. More than he'd assumed she was, but that was human history. It intertwined with the underworld from time to time but never knowingly. Vampire histories weren't written down. They couldn't be for fear of exposure. For whatever reason, Isobel desperately wanted to help, but she couldn't. It was impossible.

Smoothing down the parchment, Nye studied the meticulously scribed black ink, his gaze following the perfect lines while dread rose faster than he could contain it.

It was the same symbol that had been carved into that vampire's chest. The same symbol that was appearing all over the city. Even as he stared at it, he could feel the hint of magic the dagger and the paper were doused in, magic that reminded him of Eleanor... It was a calling card from the Unhallowed.

This was no copycat. This was the real deal, and now they were in more danger than he'd first thought. They were out for his blood, and those who stood with him would be drawn into the fold, no matter what he did. Tristan, Gabby, the Six, the London vampires...*Isobel*.

Why the parchment was stuck to his front door, written by hand rather than magically with blood, was beyond his understanding. Whatever it meant, it wasn't good.

Something bad was about to happen, and he had no idea what it was or how to stop it.

For the first time since that day in the woods near York four hundred years ago, he felt completely powerless.

Nye sat among a pile of Gabby's grimoires in the study, no closer to finding a reference to the symbol than when he'd first started.

Leaning back in his chair, he stared at the parchment like it would reveal all its secrets if he just looked hard enough. None of this made sense.

He desperately needed the assistance of a witch, but he didn't want to bring another creature in on this, especially not Sabine. She'd already asked too much for a simple barrier spell, and this would cost him a great deal more. No, this needed to be kept in-house for now. At least until Gabby returned.

There was nothing in the grimoires. Just witches nonsense that he had no way of understanding.

The symbol was undoubtedly Unhallowed in origin, but what did that star shape mean at the bottom? Did it change the intent of the magic? Or was it just their sign for 'we're coming for you.' Right now,

Nye didn't know a single thing and was resigned to wait and see.

"Nye?"

He glanced up from the desk and saw Isobel hovering in the doorway. She had her arms crossed over her stomach, a frown distorting her pretty features. Just by looking at her, he could tell she wasn't feeling well.

"Is something wrong?" he asked.

"I need to go to the store."

"No." He looked back down at the note, trying to work out its meaning.

"It's kind of important."

"No."

"I'm not a vampire like you," she hissed. "I'm a woman and things still work, you know. On a *monthly basis*."

He blinked at her, confused at her meaning, but slowly, understanding won out. "*Oh*."

She pouted. "If I'm stuck here, then you have to go for me."

Sliding the parchment into the desk drawer, he locked it inside and rose to his feet. "Fine. Tristan is downstairs. I'll make him go."

He crossed the room and stepped past her, sensing her uneasiness on the air. Her pupils dilated slightly, and she instinctively shrank away. It was her humanity picking up on his predatory nature. Ignoring the twist in his heart, he clattered down the stairs.

"While you're at it," she called after him, "get me like a million pounds of chocolate!"

He found Tristan in the lounge room watching the television intently, and Nye scowled.

It was a medieval style fantasy program that seemed to be all anyone ever talked about, and Tristan was hooked. Why he watched that rubbish was beyond him. Who had time for soap operas when they had much worse and more real threats to handle...like Isobel's womanly functions.

"Tristan," he said, picking up the remote and muting the television.

The knight raised an eyebrow at him.

"I need you to go to the supermarket for Isobel."

"Why?"

"She wants..." He waved his hands around.

"She wants?" the knight prodded.

"Don't make me say it," he snapped. "She wants female things."

Tristan's lips quirked as he tried to stifle an amused grin. "Tampons?"

"I'm not going."

"I'm not your handmaiden, Nye," he said with a chuckle. "Besides, Rajesh won't let me into his shop. You know that. He says one demon is enough. I'm not goin' all the way to Waitrose for tampons and chocolate for your human houseguest, even if she is Alex's sister."

Rajesh was the owner of the off-license down the

street. He lived above his shop, and vampires weren't allowed inside, except for Nye, which meant he had to go. "Right about now, I wish I could compel you."

"Lucky for me," Tristan said, not trying to hide his laugh.

He cursed his bad luck and stormed from the living room. If there wasn't so much going on with stupid little upstart vampires who thought they could rule the roost, then he would be able to send one of the Six to do it. He was meant to be the king, the leader of an entire city and then some, not a maid to a human woman.

But it *was* Isobel, so he went.

The off-license was two streets away near the Overground train station. The walk was a fast one, Nye's vampire feet taking him there in record time so he could get this embarrassing errand out of the way as quickly as possible.

He shoved open the door and stepped into the cool, harsh light of the fluorescent-lit store. An electronic beep signalled his arrival to the clerk behind the counter, a little, old Indian man. Rajesh. He'd owned and operated the shop for as long as Nye could remember—about thirty years give or take—and he was compelled to forget Nye and his likeness the moment he left the establishment.

Having a store that sold alcohol close by to Regulus's mansion had been handy during the last few decades. It was Nye's own private oasis of booze. Booze was liquid relaxant for vampires.

The shop itself was small, but somehow, three aisles and a bank of fridges and freezers fit inside the space. It was a miniature supermarket with the prices marked up at least thirty percent. People around here could afford the inflation, and it was all in the name of convenience for them on the way home from their dreary daily commute. For Rajesh, it was a goldmine, and one he didn't mind gouging for every last scrap it was worth.

Rajesh glanced up from the puzzle book he was working on—seemed like a Sudoku—and called out to him.

Nodding curtly, Nye went straight to the aisle he assumed stocked what Isobel needed. He stared at the selection and didn't know how women dealt with this shit. It was just as confusing and unknown to him as that stupid Unhallowed symbol he was trying to decipher.

"Lady friend, Mr. Nye?" Rajesh called out from the front counter. "I hope you don't eat her."

"No, I don't eat her." He rolled his eyes and snatched the first box that looked like it might be right. As an afterthought, he wound his way to the fridges at the back. Alcohol sounded good right about now. *Lots of alcohol.*

He ran his gaze over the rows of bottles and cans, his reflection staring back at him. Buying...*things* for a human woman. What in the world was wrong with him?

That's when he noticed someone standing in the aisle behind him. A woman in a dark hood, curly hair peeking out from underneath, her face in shadow. A spark of recognition flared in his mind as she raised her head and drew back the dark material obscuring her features.

His gaze met hers, and his heart spluttered. *No, it couldn't be.*

Spinning on his heel, he was greeted with an empty store. Looking around, he couldn't see anyone but Rajesh at the front counter still working on his Sudoku puzzle. Was it a vision or just his mind playing tricks on him? He was on edge with all the strange things going on, not to mention Isobel's presence. There was no reason *she* would be here. After all, he'd cut her head off four hundred years ago.

Eleanor.

It was another one of the Unhallowed's mind games. Perhaps that was what the symbol was for—a spell to force him to see images of his dead lover. They were sadistic, and no doubt, there would be suffering involved in this revenge plot. A great deal of it, too.

Striding to the front of the store, he tossed the items onto the counter, and Rajesh began to bag them up. Remembering that Isobel wanted chocolate, he snatched up a block of each flavour and threw them in the bag with the rest of his haul. To finish it off, he slipped Rajesh a fifty-pound note, refusing the change. The old man would forget him in less than thirty seconds anyway...at least until the next time he stopped by. Besides, money didn't hold the same value to him as it did humans.

Returning to the mansion, he flew through the foyer, ignoring Tristan's staring from the living room. He was still watching the same program as when Nye left and hadn't moved an inch. Climbing the stairs, he ventured down the hall to Isobel's room.

Wrenching open the door, he stepped inside. She was curled up on the couch, a book in her hands, and her gaze few to his. She yelped and clutched her hand to her chest, the sound of her beating heart almost overwhelming him.

"Have you ever heard of knocking?" she asked, scowling at him.

"I have your...things," he said.

She rose to her feet and tossed the book onto the coffee table, and then approached him. "That was fast."

Nye was still shaken by the vision of Eleanor he'd seen reflected in the glass of that fridge. She'd looked exactly the same as the day he'd cut off her head. Beautiful, radiant...*malicious*.

He thought he'd loved her, but that was back in a time when he was a new vampire. Everything felt more than it should then. He knew love wasn't what he'd felt for Eleanor.

He handed Isobel the plastic bag, and she took it, her fingers brushing against his. No, it wasn't love he'd felt.

"Nye..."

He shook his head, clearing the daze. "What?"

He glanced at Isobel and realised he hadn't let go of the bag. Dropping his hand away, he stepped back knowing the thoughts running through his head wouldn't amount to anything.

"What's going on, Nye?" she asked carefully. "I know it's more than a few pissed off vampires. I'm not stupid, you know."

"I didn't know what sweets you liked, so I got a bit of everything," he said, gesturing to the bag.

"Don't change the subject."

"I understand you're on edge, Isobel, but you're better off not knowing."

She stared at him, her eyes narrowing slightly like she was trying to work him out. It'd take more than a human lifetime to make sense of the mess he'd created. A lot more.

"You've changed," she finally said, looking in the bag rather than meeting his gaze.

He just frowned, wondering what she meant. He was under a lot of pressure, so maybe that's what she sensed.

"When we first met, you were...carefree, I guess.

Cracking jokes," she went on. "Now... I don't know. You're..."

"I'm who I'm meant to be," he said, trying to leave the emotion out of his voice.

"Who you're..." she scoffed and dumped the plastic bag onto the couch. "Why am I even here? It's clear you don't give a stuff, so either explain it to me or let me go. I won't be your prisoner anymore."

"You're here for your protection," he said almost robotically.

"I'm here because you're afraid of my brother."

"If I let you go, they'll kill you to spite me." The gangs of London vampires that still opposed him, the Unhallowed... They were two factions of the many he'd inherited as enemies.

"I call bullshit," Isobel declared. "Bull. Shit."

Hell, she irritated him so much. Of all the stubborn, fiery redheads to turn up on his doorstep, it had to be *her*. Isobel, who he'd been pushing away for her own good. Isobel, who was always at the back of his mind. Isobel, who smelled so sweet. *Isobel...*

Grabbing the front of her cardigan, he pulled her flush against his chest and covered her mouth with his. He kissed her with all the pent-up angst he'd been feeling since she'd appeared on his doorstep. The way she filled up everything, his head, his sight, his sense of smell, and his heart, messed with all that he was supposed to be. It was overwhelming to the point of dangerous, and he pulled back before he lost control.

"Happy?" he growled against her lips.

Isobel seemed too stunned to answer and just stared up at him with wide eyes, her heart pounding in her chest. Right about then, he wished he couldn't hear it. Letting her go, he went to stalk from the room, but she grabbed his arm, stopping him mid-stride.

"You don't understand what you're asking me to do," he murmured, casting his gaze away.

"Love a human?"

His entire body stiffened at her words. Love a human. Love Isobel. He was all wrong for her and that wasn't even considering the vampire part of the equation. The last woman he'd deigned to love had tried to kill him, and he hacked off her head. He'd started hallucinating her spirit, and the Unhallowed were rising... Isobel couldn't know about them. The more she knew, the more danger she would be in.

"Your brother wouldn't allow it, and I'm not game enough to mess with a founder, no matter how old they are," he said thinly.

"Fuck Alex," she spat, digging her fingers into him.

"He wants you to have a normal life, Isobel. Have a family. Did you forget I'm dead? That I'm a four-hundred-year-old monster? It wouldn't take much for me to lose control and hurt you." It was the truth. Even if he wasn't in a position of power, there was still the possibility of going too far in his primal lust for her blood.

"I know you, Nye. You wouldn't do that to me."

He turned on her, his eyes beginning to darken. "*You don't know me.*"

"I know you," she snarled, and he actually admired her bravery, staring right into the face of an angry vampire. "I might not know where you've been or what you've done, but I know you." She placed her hand over his heart. "I can see what's in there."

"There's nothing in there." He knocked her hands away. "Stop fooling yourself, Isobel. I will deal with the insubordinates, and then you will be free to go. You will suffer me no more."

"What's wrong with you?" she asked, shaking her head.

"On the contrary, what's wrong with *you*?" Not wanting to entertain the dangerous route the conversation was taking, he stalked from the room, slamming the door closed behind him. Leaning against the wall, he pinched the bridge of his nose.

Isobel had asked him the perfect question. What was wrong with him? He secretly cared for a human. A frail thing whose lifespan was a mere blip compared to his. The whole world had gone crazy.

He was seeing dead witches, fighting his unnatural attraction to Isobel, dealing with whoever was leaving gruesome calling cards all over London... No wonder he felt like snapping. This city needed to witness his wrath. It needed to stain the streets red.

"Nye?"

He looked up to find Tristan watching him from the other end of the hall. "What?" he snapped.

"Reed is here," he said, doing that annoying frowning thing he'd been doing ever since he returned to London. Nye got it. He was a disappointment.

"Why? He had better have an Unhallowed witch's head, or he can fuck off."

The knight shook his head. "You'd better come hear it from Reed."

"Fine."

As they walked down the stairs and away from Isobel, Tristan asked, "Is she okay?"

"Isobel is Isobel," he replied, still reeling from the taste of her lips. "Cranky and argumentative."

"I can smell her all over you," Tristan declared like a creep. "You'd better know what you're doin' with her, or Alex will rip you apart, never mind the Unhallowed."

He rolled his eyes. "I bet you peeped up girls skirts when you were a boy, Tristan."

"I didn't have time to peep," the knight replied with a chuckle. "I was too busy cleanin' up horse shit."

Stopping in the kitchen, Nye grabbed a bottle of alcohol and downed a few mouthfuls, washing away the taste of the fiery redhead upstairs. Then he opened the door to the patio and gave Tristan a look. Time to shut his mouth.

"Reed," Nye said, as the young vampire stood at their arrival. "You better have good news for me."

"Yes and no. We found the witch who strung up that vampire," he said, handing Nye his phone.

Staring at the photograph of the corpse that was once a very alive witch, he shook his head. "I've never seen this witch before. Are you sure she's responsible for the symbols?"

"As sure as we can be. We found her grimoire or what little of it she'd scribed." Reed held up a small leather-bound book and handed it to Nye. "There's only one spell inside."

"Let me guess," Nye declared, rolling his eyes. "The one that was carved into that poor sod." Flipping open the cover, he regarded the spell. The foundation for it was the same symbol that was appearing all over the city. "Did you question her before you took her head?"

"We weren't given a chance," Reed explained. "We cornered her in a back alley, but at the last second, we realised it was a trap. Her wards rendered the others immobile, but I was able to slip through. I had to kill her, or we'd all go down." He bowed his head. "I'm sorry, sir."

Nye snorted, remembering his various run-ins with witches over the decades. "You made the right decision."

"The grimoire isn't much to go on," Tristan said, taking it from Nye. "It can't verify anything."

"The thing is," Reed said. "We decided to try mapping the locations of the symbols to see if they meant anything. I've seen something like it before where on a larger scale the hotspots are part of a grander design." He tapped on the screen of his phone and gave it back to Nye. "It's not a design but... I think it's a *route*."

Nye's eyes widened as his gaze followed the points the symbol had carved through the city. All the way from Cheapside where they'd found the corpse...to *Hampstead*.

The witch the Six had beheaded was planted. The Unhallowed wanted Nye to know they were coming. The symbol on the door...now he understood. It wasn't a warning or a sadistic party invite. It was a *target*.

"Get me Sabine," he barked at Tristan. "*Now*."

"What's—"

"Whatever the Unhallowed have planned, it's coming to us," he said, interrupting the knight's questioning. "I don't know when or what, but something is being led here. Something that's coming for us all."

"Something?" Tristan asked. "Like what?"

"Fucked if I know, but we need to fortify the mansion. *Get me Sabine*." Turning to Reed, he commanded, "Bring the Six and anyone you can spare. The Unhallowed cannot be allowed to take the mansion."

The vampire nodded, and in a gust of air, he disappeared with Tristan not far behind. All that was left to do was to wait until the knight brought him the witch. When she arrived, the real work would begin.

Glancing up at the light filtering down from Isobel's bedroom window, Nye's blood began to thrum. What had he done by forcing her to remain here? If this went badly, she'd die along with them all. Had he condemned her to a fate worse than death? Was that how loving a vampire would truly end?

Going back inside, he stormed into the kitchen and wrenched open the fridge. Grabbing a bag of blood, he ripped open the tab at the top and gulped down the entire thing before snatching another.

The Unhallowed were coming, and he'd need his strength if he was going to beat them.

CHAPTER 8

Nye strode upstairs to Isobel's room. Of all the nights for the Unhallowed to rear their ugly heads...

"Isobel," he cried, whirlwinding into the bedroom.

"Nye," she said, rising to her feet. "What's wrong?" Her pretty brown eyes were wide, full of confusion and something else...hope that he'd changed his mind about their interlude moments before, perhaps.

He shook his head and closed his heart off. "Lock yourself in this room, and do not come out. *For anything.* You hear me?"

Her expression fell. "What's going on?"

"*Stay in here.*"

"*Nye!*" she exclaimed as he slammed the door closed behind him, shutting her inside the room.

She'd be safe in the house, and once Sabine had done her magical juju, nothing the Unhallowed threw at them would be able to come inside and harm her. At least, he hoped that was the case.

Downstairs, he waited for the cavalry. Reed had been well prepared, and the Six turned up in record time. He'd brought along another six of their closest friends, so there were twelve vampires assembled, waiting to assist in the fight—thirteen if he counted himself.

"Whatever this attack is, it's a threat to us all," Nye snarled. "They won't stop at me. Once they take the mansion, the city will be next. The London vampires will die if we don't stop this."

He had no doubt that's what they were after, and making it known to the Six and their friends was a logical step in cementing his place as leader. If he died, then it was only a matter of time before the rest fell.

"We'll surround the mansion," Felixstowe said.

"If anything comes at us, we'll know about it long before it crosses the property line," Fox added.

"There are twelve of us," Reed declared. "Two to a team should suffice. Sir?"

Nye nodded, impressed with the work the young vampire had done in the last few days. He was a keeper. "Spread out, but not too far from one another in case you're needed. I will remain here until Tristan arrives with the witch." The Six began to look uneasy, and he could barely contain his annoyance. "*Time to fight fire with fire.*"

The Six and the other assembled vampires moved

away to take their positions, leaving Nye standing on the patio alone to stare out across the garden.

His vampire eyes took in the sharp lines of the olive tree growing strongly at the rear, the tree Gabby had planted over Regulus's body and had grown with her magic. Was he doing the right thing? Standing here, picking up the frayed threads of the Roman's rule while trying to find his place in this screwed-up world...

He remembered the intensity of his feelings for Eleanor like it was yesterday. Over the years, he'd pushed her to the back of his mind, but the witch had always been a part of his story, no matter what he did to try to forget. Thinking about Isobel and how things had spiralled out of control in such a short amount of time, he knew what he felt for her burned so bright it dulled the Unhallowed witch to nothing.

Why did it have to be Isobel?

Movement at his right pulled his attention as an inky shadow leapt from the darkness and collided with him. He fell to the ground with the thing on top of him, a mess of arms and legs. *He didn't even hear it!*

Realising it was a man, Nye grabbed his shoulders and shoved him back. His eyes widened in surprise as he beheld the face of the vampire who had been hanging in the construction site in Cheapside. The vampire's desiccated flesh was rotting, clumps falling away from the bone instead of turning into the hard leather his dried out corpse should have had in death.

What the hell?

"*Nye!*"

Reed's voice pulled the creature's attention, and Nye took the moment of distraction and turned it to his advantage. Pushing with all his strength, the corpse fell backward, and Nye got to his feet, but it wasn't for long.

The creature was back with a vengeance. Whatever magic had brought it to life was making it stronger than it had ever been while it was a vampire. It was a zombified lump of flesh with no intelligent thought patterns, which meant it felt no pain. Supercharged with magic, it was the perfect killing machine.

"Rip its head off!" Nye roared as it lunged for him.

Vampires emerged from the shadows, drawn by the commotion, and the creature stopped and turned. It was surrounded by some of the best men and women the London vampires had to offer. There was no way it was getting out of here without its head detached from its body.

Its mouth opened, revealing a row of sharpened fangs, and it began wailing. Then before any of them understood what was happening, it struck. Faster than even Nye's eyes could follow, it put down each one of the surrounding vampires, the circle collapsing like dominos.

In one fluid motion, the creature had put down twelve vampires, and its eerie gaze locked onto Nye. Where the hell was Tristan with Sabine?

"You want me, huh?" he asked, and its head tilted to the side like it was listening. "You tell Eleanor and her witch friends they'll have to try harder than this."

The creature shot forward, its hand curling around Nye's neck, and he was lifted clear off the ground. Without so much as a word or a moan, the corpse threw him to the side. Nye landed on the paved patio in a lump, expecting the creature to try to kill him, but he rolled over to nothing...

The creature wailed and slammed against the window, the force shattering the glass, which exploded into tiny granules and rained down onto the patio and all over the kitchen beyond. It hurled itself inside and disappeared into the cavernous house.

Reed glanced at Nye, a fearful expression on his face. *The Six couldn't get in.*

Nye pushed to his feet and flew into the house, following the rotten stench the creature had left in its wake. The sound of wood splintering pulled his attention to the east side of the building, and then a blood-curdling scream tore apart the air.

Isobel!

Nye ran up the stairs as fast as his vampire feet could take him, searing anger controlling his every move as he rushed through the broken door to her bedroom. Stumbling, he saw the creature poised to lunge at a petrified Isobel as she cowered against the far wall.

Her gaze met his, and it was full of a fear he hadn't

seen in a very long time. The fear of imminent death with so much left unsaid.

He didn't have a choice. There was none as far as he was concerned. He had to save her, no matter the cost.

Nye leapt into action, throwing himself onto the creature's back. It thrashed, turning them away from where Isobel was pinned against the wall. It shook Nye loose, and he stumbled before launching himself at it again.

Its flesh was peeling away from its body at an alarming rate—whatever spell brought it here was starting to decay—and he couldn't grab hold of it long enough to subdue its thrashing. Finally, he caged its back against his chest, attempting to smash its putrid head against the wall.

Isobel screamed and scuttled further back into the corner, her hands fumbling for something to defend herself with, but there was nothing to grab.

Whirling around, Nye was trying to pull the creature from the room to save her from a front row seat to a rotting, zombified, vampire's dismemberment when he saw Tristan standing in the doorway, a look of shock on his face.

"*Tristan!*" he roared as he struggled to keep his hold on the thrashing corpse.

The knight darted forward and grasped its head, but before he could twist, it kicked out at him, his feet colliding with the knight's stomach, sending him clear across the room and out into the hall.

Just as Nye's grip was slipping, he felt power thrum through the air, and the creature jerked and went slack, its tongue lolling out the side of its mouth. Glancing up, his gaze met Sabine's, and she nodded once. Nye snarled, ripping the head clean off the creature's neck and not a moment too soon.

Tristan stumbled back into the room and stared at the corpse. "*What the hell?*"

"Get it out of here," Sabine said to them and then glanced at Isobel. "I'll make sure she's all right."

Nye cast a concerned glance at Isobel, but she was staring at the creature and the mess it'd left behind on the floor.

Tristan knelt down, tossed the head onto the pile of body parts, and began to roll the entire thing up in the expensive Persian rug it'd ruined.

Nye glanced at Isobel, not knowing what to say. She was white as a sheet, her heart beating so fast...

"Nye," Tristan said, prodding him into action.

Leaving the women behind, they carried the remains downstairs and out onto the patio.

The house was a mess. Gabby would be furious they'd messed up the window and the carpets of a house she'd only owned for a few weeks. Even Regulus didn't fight at home. No, the founder had the foresight and cunning to be able to pick his locations. *What a shambles.*

When Sabine returned, Nye was leaning against the side of the house, trembling with restrained fury and smelling like rotting flesh. He was covered in congealed zombie blood and guts, but he didn't care about that right now. He'd gathered Tristan and the Six and sent them out to scour the grounds and surrounding streets for signs of the Unhallowed and any more creatures they may have created, but his mind was on Isobel.

He glanced up at the witch, who smiled knowingly. If she had anything to say about the fact the leader of the London vampires had a thing for a human woman, she didn't say it aloud.

"She's shaken up, but she'll be okay in time," she said.

"What exactly was that thing?" he asked.

Sabine shrugged. "It's hard to say exactly, but the spell Tristan showed me... I've never seen anything like it. It's dark that much I know. I'm guessing the overall symbol is of the coven it was cast by, but I've never come across it. The star at the base of the central line... I've seen it used in necromancy. It's an embellishment that changes the intent of a spell."

Nye jabbed a finger at what was left of the creature on the patio beside them. "Considering we saw that guy strung up and dead as a door nail the other night, it's safe to say he was reanimated."

Sabine stared at the corpse. After a moment, she declared, "I can't tell how it was created, but it wasn't with earth magic. If it was another element, I would be able to pick up clues... This is new."

"Spirit magic?" he asked, knowing a witch's magic was inherited from their bloodlines. Each founding witch had an affinity with a certain element and it was passed down. It was a rare witch who was descended from the fifth element, which was the ether, the spirit, and it was another reason he wished Gabby was here. She was the most powerful witch he'd even known. She was of the ether and could walk within the spirit realm.

"It's possible," Sabine replied. "I've never known a witch who could wield power like that, so I can't say for sure."

"How was it able to get into the house?"

"It's not a vampire anymore. Death took that binding from his body," the witch explained. "As far as I can tell, he's a soulless corpse and can be commanded to go anywhere."

Closing his eyes, he cursed under his breath. Then Isobel wasn't safe here. She wasn't safe anywhere unless he could do something to stop the Unhallowed at the source. "Can you place a ward to stop any more of these things getting inside?"

"I'll need to examine the creature before I can."

"Then do it."

She smiled and fluttered her eyelashes at him. "It will cost you, Nye."

"Name the amount," he said with a sigh.

Her gaze dropped, raking over his body. "Who said anything about money?"

Nye straightened up and curled his lip. "I do not barter with sex."

She smiled in triumph, and then her eyes narrowed dangerously. "So you do love her."

"Name the amount, Sabine, or leave," he snarled, knowing he'd just unwittingly given the witch a powerful secret to use against him.

"Fifty thousand," she declared, her pride clearly hurt. "Next time, it doubles."

As promised and paid for, Sabine cast wards around the mansion grounds. The spells wouldn't keep the creatures out, but if they came knocking again, they'd get enough warning to stop them before they got inside.

It was her parting gift that had him worried. On her way out, Sabine had joyfully declared the creature wasn't there just to kill but to siphon energy. It was just like Eleanor had tried to do to him the day Nye had killed her. The Unhallowed were trying to finish what she'd started.

Anyway, he could no longer count on asking Sabine for help. She knew too much, and if she knew Isobel's relationship to Alex, then he was in even more trouble than he already was.

In the hard light of day, the house looked like a bomb had gone off in it. Tristan had compelled some workmen to fix the damage, and for the better part of the afternoon, there'd been sounds of hammering filling the furthest reaches of the grounds.

Isobel had hidden herself away in the study while her room was cleaned and repaired, which had sent Nye to the patio. He wasn't in the mood to be in the same room as the human woman he'd kissed and almost killed in the space of half an hour. He sure as hell didn't trust himself to be alone with her.

The entire patio and house still stunk like rotting flesh, and the scent stuck up his nose. It was just another thing on a long list of failings and annoyances that had ruled his afterlife the last two weeks.

Tristan returned later that night as Nye sat on the patio watching the stars come out. If there were a time he missed having his best mate, Zac, around, it was now. Zac and his girl, Aya, would know what to do. Aya was a witch hunter and would be able to sniff out the Unhallowed in no time. Problem with that was he didn't know where in the world they were or how to contact them. Anyway, he was loath to call for help when he was supposed to have the power to deal with these issues himself.

"Tell me you have good news," he said as the knight sat beside him on the ledge.

"The damage has been fixed," Tristan replied, sitting a can of air freshener next to him. *Smartass.*

Nye snorted, not taking the bait.

"Isobel has returned to her room and has been askin' after you."

"I bet she has," he replied, the memory of kissing her still the brightest memory in his mind. "What else?"

"The Six have found somethin' down in Vauxhall."

He sighed and glanced at Tristan. "What and when?"

"Another body turned up a half hour ago. Reed is there containing the area."

"Good old Reed," Nye said with a sneer.

"He's a good soldier," Tristan said, raising his eyebrows. "The perfect choice for the Six."

Nye snorted. "Give me the location, and I'll meet them immediately."

Tristan pulled out his phone and texted the information, and a moment later, his own phone vibrated as the message arrived.

"Someone needs to stay here with Isobel," he said, glancing over his shoulder into the kitchen. "I don't want to leave the mansion unattended."

"I'll stay," Tristan said. "I'm the only one who's invited in."

"Good." Nye rose to his feet. "See that she's taken care of."

Before Tristan could partake in any more unwanted tidbits of advice, he disappeared into the darkness, bound for Vauxhall and the newest Unhallowed calling card.

Vauxhall was a district of London that sat on the south bank of the Thames, directly upstream of Westminster with its grand Houses of Parliament.

From his position on the embankment, Nye could see the glow of Big Ben and the shape of another corpse at his feet.

As if an ex-vampire zombie wasn't enough excitement for the week, another body had turned up. This time, over the site of a medieval era graveyard that was now nothing more than an empty lot with a concrete slab over the top.

Nye remembered this place, its history having gone back further than he was alive. When he was a new vampire, he remembered this place as a burial ground for the outcasts of society—criminals, the insane, the sick, and the unwanted. They were all thrown into mass graves that now lay beneath their feet. London was full of places like this. Places that time forgot and the modern world had built over—tombs at old churches, plague pits, pauper's graves, hospital burial grounds...and all of them hotspots for spiritual power that the Unhallowed snacked on like peanuts at a pub.

That was why Nye wasn't surprised to find a body with a carved up chest here.

Reed stood beside him while the rest of the Six scoured the site for any clues they may have missed. The young vampire was fast becoming their leader, and Nye was glad he'd chosen him as one of his elite.

"How was this one positioned?" he asked.

"Flat on his back with his arms and legs splayed out like a star," Reed replied. "He was in the centre of the lot."

So they were using the remnants of energy that had been accumulating over the centuries. From the things he'd heard from witches over the years, the magic they siphoned here would be dark, the lives the dead had lived tainting the earth they'd been buried in. So it lived up to the Unhallowed's refined tastes for pure evil, then.

"This one is different," Reed went on, kneeling by the body. "The star is replaced with this curved line." The tip of his finger followed the marking. "I wonder what this one is for..."

"I'd rather not wait and see," Nye said. "Burn the body to ash. Let's see it try to reanimate then."

"Understood."

"We need to stay on high alert," he continued. "Watch your backs. Unfortunately, this isn't over."

"Don't worry, sir," Reed said. "We'll figure it out. You're doing what you can. The vampires will understand it in time."

"Are you questioning my strength?" he asked, glaring at the vampire. He liked the man, but he was becoming much too familiar. In his position, Nye couldn't afford to be friends with the men he commanded or have them think he was faltering.

Reed's eyes widened, and he shook his head. "No, of course not."

"Then you have your orders." He glanced at the corpse, his lip curling into a sneer. "See that they're carried out."

CHAPTER 9

Isobel sat on the couch in her room, staring at the place the Persian rug used to be.

When she closed her eyes, she could still see the image of the bloated corpse hurling itself across the room. The stench had been horrible, sweet and sickly like a peach that had been left out in the sun to rot. She shivered at the memory of the wail that came from its mouth as it launched itself at her. Nye appeared without so much as a second to spare before it had her in its clutches.

Drawing aimlessly in the notebook sitting in her lap, her thoughts went to the vampire. If she concentrated hard enough, she could almost feel the moment he'd kissed her. *Almost*.

She'd positioned herself on the couch so she could see the bedroom door, which was all new and shiny. One thing she'd realised after that creature had burst in here was that she wasn't entirely safe. A magical barrier trapped her inside, but it wasn't impenetrable. Other things besides vampires could get in…

So when the door opened and Nye appeared, she saw him without having to look up from the doodle she was working on. Her heart didn't flip, and her skin didn't tingle. She was far too shaken to dwell on a vampire's hasty kiss.

"I was wondering if you were going to show up," she said, her pen scratching over the paper.

"I'm sorry it wasn't sooner."

She dug the pen harder into the paper as she worked on perfecting the edge of the circle. She'd seen the symbol sliced into the zombie's torso clear as day and like its face, she couldn't get it out of her mind.

"Duty called?" she retorted, glancing up at the vampire.

Nye shuffled, looking uncomfortable for once. "I had to make sure…"

Looking at her rough sketch, she frowned. Was this what everyone saw on that bit of paper stuck to the front door yesterday? The thing only supernatural eyes could see?

Holding up the notebook, she turned it around so Nye could see. "Is this it?" she asked. "The thing that was on that note?"

He glanced at the sketch and then at her. His eyes told the story his mouth didn't vocalise. It was the symbol, which meant it had something to do with magic. It was a spell of some kind and probably one that made that dead body move again.

Isobel sighed and tossed the notebook onto the coffee table. "I have eyes, you know. I can see things like rotting zombies that try to kill me."

"Isobel..." Nye stepped closer but still didn't move to sit down. "You shouldn't have to be involved in this. I didn't know... I didn't know what was coming."

"I can do something," she said, sitting up straighter. "Right now, I'm just a useless lump. A liability locked away in a corner."

"You were attacked last night," he said.

"I have a Masters in Anthropology, Sociology, and Ancient Literature," she declared. She knew things that might be helpful or at least had an objective mind that could work things out if she didn't.

"So?"

"If these witches have left a trail through story or history, I can find it. I can find out where they came from and when. Something in their story might lead you to a way to stop them."

"You can, or you might?" he asked. "They are two very different things."

"If it's there, I can find it, but I need access."

His eyes narrowed, and he shook his head. "You cannot leave the house, Isobel. Nice try, though."

Her heart sank. "But I can help you!"

"Perhaps, but here, I can protect you."

"Nice way of protecting me last night," she said with a pout.

"How do you know it was witches? Have you been eavesdropping?"

Isobel scoffed as Nye finally sat on the couch next to her. "How can I eavesdrop when you have super hearing? You'd hear me lurking, no matter how silent I thought I was being. Anyway..." She pointed at the symbol. "Why carve that into a corpse unless it had something to do with the fact *it could move*."

Nye's lips began to curve into a smile. "You're more perceptive than I gave you credit for."

"What's going on, Nye? After last night, I think you owe me an explanation."

His eyes narrowed. "They're a coven of witches called the Unhallowed."

"The Unhallowed? That doesn't sound ominous in the least."

"I wronged them back in the early sixteen hundreds, and they aren't the kind of people who give up on a grudge."

"After four hundred years, I'd say that's obsessive compulsive more than anything," she said, screwing up her nose. "Wronged how? It must've been a doozy if they sent a zombie after you."

"I killed the daughter of their matriarch."

Isobel's eyes widened, and she snorted. "That'd do it."

"It was a case of kill or be killed," he said, looking

uncomfortable. "Regulus helped... She was about to kill me and siphon my energy... Regulus freed me and allowed me my revenge."

"So that's why you hung around him for so long?"

He nodded. "Back then... I was lost. I didn't... I didn't have a purpose, and he gave me a reason to be what I became."

"A vampire?" she asked carefully, knowing it was highly likely Nye had never wanted to turn in the first place.

"Yes." His gaze lowered. "If you know one thing about me, Isobel, know that I never chose this life."

Her heart twisted, and she shifted closer. She wanted to take his hand in hers to give him at least a tiny sliver of comfort, but the fact he'd never deliberately touched her outside of their kiss had her hesitating.

"If you weren't here..." Nye said out of nowhere. "If you'd never met us... What would you be doing?"

Isobel frowned. She could scarcely remember what she wanted anymore. A few days ago, she would've said she wanted to marry an archaeologist and travel the world having adventures deep in the Amazon jungle... but now? Life seemed richer closer to home. There was this whole world full of fantastical, albeit dangerous, creatures with their own histories and stories.

"I'm not sure I want that anymore," she replied. "I had it all planned out... I can't see it anymore."

"Then what do you want now?"

She shrugged.

"When you go to bed at night and it's dark and you're in your own secret world...who do you dream about?"

Who did she dream about? What was he trying to say?

"Nye—"

He shook his head before she could ask. "Answer the question, Isobel."

Why was he even asking her this? Was he trying to help her find a path away from him, her brother, and the whole vampire world? Now that she was among the chaos, she'd never be able to stop thinking about it. Unless he was about to compel her to forget. Vampires could do that.

"Don't," she said, jerking away.

Nye frowned. "Don't what?"

"Don't compel me."

"Then tell me what you want, Isobel. What. Do. You. *Want*?"

"You," she said with a sigh, sick and tired of pretending. "I dream about you."

His gaze flickered to her lips and back up. "Nightmares."

She frowned, not understanding how he could keep pushing her away. She understood what he was, *who* he was.

"Your dreams are nightmares," he said with more force.

He wasn't getting away with it this time. She raised a steady hand and let her fingertips brush against the puckered tip of his scar, her gaze following their movement. Nye didn't move or jerk away as she reached the bridge of his nose. He just sat there, watching...waiting to see what she'd do.

Her fingers traced the scar through his eyebrow, and his eyes fluttered closed. He seemed to have more self-control than she did, she'd give him that.

"Isobel," he murmured. "I'm not good for you."

"Shh," she crooned, shifting closer.

His hand shot up and grasped her wrist, pulling her away from her tentative exploration. "Stop."

"I don't want to."

"Isobel..."

She moved closer, her body drawn by the mixed feelings she had toward him. She knew she was tempting fate, but she couldn't stop herself even if she tried.

Nye's grasp slackened, and her wrist slipped through his hand until her fingers entwined with his. His skin was cool to the touch, his palm calloused and rough from the human life he'd led as a spy and soldier for the English in the sixteenth century.

His eyes were a brilliant shade of earthy brown, dark around the outside and fading to a bright hazel in the centre. Despite the scar that divided his face, he was handsome. No, not handsome. *Beautiful.*

Leaning closer, Nye's hand dropped from hers and

curled around her waist. Then before she could gather her thoughts, his lips pressed against hers. Softly at first, but then as awareness washed over her, she increased the pressure, winding her arms around his neck like she would any other man she was attracted to. Nye was no ordinary man, but where there was lust, sense went straight out the window.

He deepened their embrace, tugging her onto his lap as her lips parted to allow him control. His taste filled her human senses, making her giddy, and absently, she wondered if this was one of his vampire tricks. He was rather good at kissing.

Her blood thrummed through her veins, pleasure building in all the right places as his tongue twined with hers. Faster and harder until she moaned deeply, never wanting him to stop. It felt so good... She'd never been kissed like this before, like she was the most desirable thing in the world, and it felt extraordinary.

Before she could take another breath, Nye pushed her gently back onto the couch, positioning his body over hers. His lips moved along her jaw, skimming along her neck where he laid a thousand more kisses against her skin.

Extraordinary.

She was lost to the longing his touch had awakened in her when she felt him bite down...*hard.* Her eyes flew open as pain shot through her neck. Her heart began to race as understanding washed over her, dousing the passion she'd allowed to rule her body. He was... *He was feeding on her!*

She felt the blood leaving her body, and she began to panic, writhing against him, but she was held tightly with no chance of escape. He'd tried to tell her...

"*Nye*," she cried. "Nye, stop... Please..."

He didn't reply, and she suspected he was lost to the taste of her blood as he drank.

What was she meant to do? Her gaze fell onto the notebook and pen that sat on the coffee table beside her. Desperate times called for desperate measures.

Fumbling for the pen, her fingers curled tightly around it and she stabbed, slamming the pointed end into his neck with as much strength as she could gather. It was either that or end up... Well, she didn't want to finish that thought.

Instantly, Nye let go and fell back onto the couch with a cry, his hand clutching at the pen that protruded from his flesh. Isobel scuttled backward, her hand closing over her throbbing skin. Beginning to tremble violently, she pulled her fingers away and stared at the blood that coated them. *Her blood.*

Nye hissed as he pulled the pen out, his gaze meeting hers, and seeing his black eyes and bloodstained face, she realised he was right. He'd warned her time and time again about what he was and the things he was capable of doing to her. *He'd warned her.*

Still, even though his eyes were total darkness, she could see the regret and pain in them. "*Isobel...*"

He moved, and she jerked away instinctively, almost falling onto the floor. "You... You..."

He thrust his hands into his hair and moaned like he was in pain. "What have I done?"

He rose to his feet and stared at her, despair written all over his handsome features. His mouth opened and closed, and finally, he strode from the room faster than her gaze could follow.

The door slammed closed, and she was left to curl up on the couch and cry, her neck throbbing.

She was in the bathroom, poking at the teeth marks in her neck when Tristan appeared behind her.

Thankfully, he'd made his presence known before entering. Otherwise, she would've stabbed him as well.

Nye had disappeared, leaving her to seethe in his absence. He'd been trying to tell her the risks, but she wouldn't listen. Her heart was screaming in her ear to kiss him, to let him have what he wanted, to give her pleasure, and he lived up to all the sinister promises he'd been making since she had arrived.

Despite it all, there was still a part of her that wanted to keep pushing. There had to be some kind of light at the end of all this darkness, right? If there wasn't, what was the point of anything? Of life...or what came after death.

At least she'd had the guts to stab Nye in the neck. That was a new level of violence for her.

Glancing at Tristan's reflection, she sighed.

"Are you okay?" the vampire asked.

"It stings," she replied, not elaborating any further.

"Come," he said, gesturing for her to turn around. "I can help you with that."

She turned just as he stuck his thumb into his mouth and bit. His eyes began to mist over much like Nye's had, and she fell back against the marble bench-top.

"You have nothin' to fear from me, Isobel," he said, holding out his thumb. "My blood will clear this right up. May I?"

She swallowed and calmed herself. "Okay."

"Tilt your head to the side."

She did as he commanded, hissing as he placed his thumb against the bite marks and began massaging his blood into the wound.

"This isn't kinky at all," she declared as the knight stroked her skin.

Tristan laughed softly and continued until the sting had subsided. "All done. Do you feel better?"

Turning, she peeked into the mirror and found her skin was completely healed, though she desperately needed a shower to get rid of the excess red stuff.

"Incredible," she breathed.

"It does come in handy in a tight spot," the knight replied, moving back into the bedroom. "Do you require anythin' else? I can leave you to wash up..."

Isobel hesitated, wondering if questioning Tristan about Nye's feelings was appropriate considering the two men's relationship. She got the distinct impression they'd loathed one another for a long time, and current circumstances was the only thing holding them together.

In the end, curiosity won out.

"Hey, can I ask you for some advice?" she asked, moving back to the couch in the bedroom. *The scene of the crime.*

Tristan inclined his head and sat beside her. "To a point, I suppose."

"You're a thousand-year-old vampire," she said. "What do you think about all of this? Nye and..." She swallowed, averting her gaze. "Me."

Tristan leaned back into the arm of the couch. "Well, for starters, vampires feel things a hundred times deeper than a human. It's why many of us choose to turn that part of ourselves off."

Isobel frowned. "What do you mean 'off'? Just like a light switch?"

The knight nodded. "It sounds callous, I know, but some vampires could never cope with their emotions in their human lives, so imagine that feelin' of helplessness amplified."

Her mouth formed an 'O' as she began to understand. "Nye?"

"He still has his," he said with a chuckle. "Though sometimes I wish he'd tone it down."

"He can be intense under the smartass exterior, right?"

Tristan laughed. "Yes, that's true."

Isobel cast her gaze away, picking at the drying blood on her fingers. Perhaps this was Tristan's roundabout way of explaining why Nye had lost control and bitten her. Maybe he couldn't help it because of the things he felt for her. She was too afraid of acknowledging that a vampire might love her. If that were true, then he'd always love her more deeply that she would ever be able to love him. Not to mention the getting old part.

"I've known Nye most of his vampire life," Tristan said after a moment. "He lives very much in a grey area, Isobel. Neither good nor bad."

"Is that code for him being in it for himself?" she asked with a roll of her eyes.

Tristan's lips curled into a grin. "Sometimes, but I think he struggles when it comes to you."

That was the part she was hoping Tristan would skim over, but it was also the part she wanted to know the most.

"If he would let me go home, he wouldn't have to deal with it anymore."

"Do you really want to leave?"

Isobel glanced up, meeting Tristan's eerie gaze. Vampires were kind of creepy with their low blink ratio.

If she was being honest with herself, then a part of her wanted to stay. If she was aiming for self-preservation, then she wanted to go back to her life in Oxford, finish her Masters, and go on to travel and research her way into old age. Perhaps she would marry an archaeologist and have fabulous adventures discovering ancient secrets together. That was what she'd once dreamed about—the dream she'd forgotten while being beguiled by Nye Saer—but then one night, Gabby Cohen had knocked on her door and changed everything.

Isobel could only shrug. How could she vocalise that to a man she hardly knew?

"Nye is hard on himself," Tristan said, frowning at her response. "I've never seen him care for a woman before."

"You think he cares for me?" she asked, blinking hard. "And here I was thinking it was only a physical thing."

"To put it bluntly, Nye could've healed you himself and compelled the memory away, but he didn't do that, did he?"

She felt her cheeks heat and stared down at her hands. This conversation had done nothing but confuse her further...and give her many more things to blow out of proportion and overthink in her isolation.

"You should clean up," Tristan said, rising to his feet. "The blood becomes distractin' after a while."

"Oh," she exclaimed, sitting up straight. "I didn't realise... I'm sorry."

"It's okay," the knight said with a wink. "I'm much better at this than most. You've nothin' to worry about."

"Well, it's clear I still have a lot to learn."

"You will understand in time," the knight replied, materialising by the door. "As well as you are able."

"You're really wise, you know that?"

Tristan laughed and eased open the door. "Some would say otherwise, but a vampire never forgets the definin' moments of their human life. Sleep well, Isobel."

She smiled as he disappeared, beginning to feel much better about the night's events. Nye had bitten her in a moment of passion, but Tristan had put it into perspective. Well, as much perspective as her human mind could understand.

Chivalry wasn't dead...it was just *un*dead.

CHAPTER 10

The dark streets of London had become familiar to Tristan over the years.

He'd worked in much the same position beside Regulus as he did Nye, and the city held a long-lost nostalgia when it came to his days as a squire for the Knights Templar. Of course, it was much changed, the players in his life long dead and buried, but the memories remain, clinging to the land like some kind of spiritual residue.

Arrow, or Aya as she was known, had told him that once. The raven-haired woman who was unable to trick the human knight into thinking she was a man like the rest of their unit on the long road to Istanbul. Lady Arrow. The name had stuck long after she'd disappeared from his life. She was the one who'd taught him all he knew about being a vampire and witch hunter. She'd never returned his love, and that was a part of himself he'd only come to terms with recently. A thousand years was a long time dead.

Turning his attention to the modern streets around him, he kept his senses sharp as he searched for the calling cards that told him the Unhallowed were lurking.

The breeze picked up the closer he ventured toward the Thames and with it, the wind brought a telltale scent.

Turning his head, Tristan breathed deeply. This time, he got a good whiff of the stench and screwed up his nose. It wasn't just rotting flesh he detected because it all smelt the same. No, it had a definite tang that told him it was something more. He remembered it from the other night when that creature had forced its way into the mansion.

Altering his course down the side alley, he kept his senses alert and eyes sharp. They were at a disadvantage considering they knew next to nothing about the witches, and any clue was worth its weight in metaphoric gold right now, so Tristan followed his nose.

There was no way of telling what the symbol on the second corpse was for or if they had in fact stopped the spell from playing out. As Nye had commanded, Reed had burned the body into ash and tipped what was left into the Thames. It was quite possible they'd thwarted the Unhallowed this time. This time, because there was no doubt there would be a third attempt and a fourth and fifth...

Then there was the fact that Nye had lost control and bitten Isobel. If anything, he'd seen it coming, but there was no telling Nye. The spy had reminded Tristan of his position many times already. Whatever advice he had about Isobel wasn't wanted, and when it came to vampire-human relationships, he didn't want to get involved in the inevitable fallout.

The problem was he genuinely liked Isobel. She was strong, independent, and didn't take any nonsense from Nye. Perhaps in another lifetime, they would have been good for one another. Who knew.

Turning down another side alley, he caught the scent again—only this time, stronger.

An unseen force slammed into his stomach, and he stumbled. Then he was moved back against the wall, his head cracking against the brick. Realising he'd stepped into a witch's web of wards, he tried to twist out of the way, but his movements were becoming more sluggish as he struggled. His body was sucked to the ground like he was being swallowed whole by quicksand, and he fell flat onto his back. He stared up at the sky, unable to move, no matter how hard he tried to struggle.

A figure appeared over him, haloed in the light of the moon that hung over their position. Narrowing his eyes, he realised it was a woman. The witch who'd planted the trap he's stupidly walked right into.

"Tristan na Tri Tor," she said, standing over him, his eye drawn to the dagger in her hand that was glinting in the moonlight.

So it appeared he was next on the list. *Lucky number three.*

He looked the woman over regarding her long, curly, brown hair and deceitful eyes and saw darkness inside her soul. He'd been walking the earth a very long time and much of that was spent beside the hybrid Aya, the infamous Witch Hunter, tracking down and putting an end to evil. Tristan knew a great deal about the way witches operated and the magic that corrupted them. This woman...she reeked with the stench of death.

"It's too bad," she purred, her hands pulling at his jumper. "You're cute, but you're positioned right where I need you to be—the right hand of my murderer. Yes, you'll do just fine."

"You're Eleanor," he said as the tip of her knife trailed along his stomach.

"The word dead has such a finality about it," she replied, blowing him a kiss. "Nothing truly dies, Tristan, least of all an Unhallowed witch."

She didn't deny her identity, but he supposed she was confident he was done for. While he still drew breath, there was always hope.

"Why now?" he asked, trying to move against the invisible bonds that held him. "Four hundred years is a long time to wait in the shadows."

She smiled. "All good things take time."

"Have you been alive all this time?" He didn't understand how she could be here. Not even Aya had known of a spell that could prolong a witch's life beyond a hundred or so years.

"You know so much yet understand so little," Eleanor replied, straddling his prone body. Holding the knife in two hands, she drove the tip into his skin, pain beginning to burn his flesh. He could feel the power traveling from her, through the steel, and into him.

He would not end up like the corpses that had been appearing around the city. He wouldn't allow her to turn him into a reanimated sack of rotting flesh sent to tear his friends apart. Not after all of the things he'd seen in this world. He couldn't become a part of the feral darkness that had taken him all those long years ago. There was no way in hell.

He felt her knife carving into the flesh of his chest, the symbol coming closer to completion, and he pushed against her with all eleven hundred years of his accumulated strength.

Her eyes widened in surprise as he broke free of her hold, and suddenly, he was shoving her aside. Baring his fangs, he dove onto her and tore into her neck. Eleanor screamed as the knife clattered to the cobblestones, the sound hardly registering as her blood began to burn his mouth and throat rather than fill him with the strength he needed to take her out.

Letting her go, he clutched his neck, spitting blood all over the ground. It was eating through his flesh like acid...

Eleanor began to laugh hysterically as she lay flat on her back. "Tastes nice, doesn't it?"

Tristan heaved, throwing up the contents of his stomach. What in the world was happening?

Slowly, the witch sat up, her expression falling from laughter into darkness. He felt the crackle of static charging the air, and he knew he had to do something or bear the brunt of the spell the witch was muttering under her breath.

His throat burned, his stomach hissing and spitting inside of him as her blood ate away at his flesh, and Tristan knew he couldn't fight her. Not alone and not without a witch to help him. The only thing he could do if he wanted to get out of this and warn Nye was to run.

Stumbling to his feet, he slammed against the wall, his balance thrown off. Eleanor's hands rose as the spell began to crescendo, and he ran.

Emerging onto the street, he heard her enraged cry behind him and the sound of running feet as she attempted pursuit. No doubt, she'd hoped the poison that was her blood would subdue him long enough to complete her ritual. *Not tonight.*

Tristan turned and ran, not stopping until he burst through the front door of the mansion. Climbing the stairs, he shoved into the study and fell to his knees as Nye rose to his feet.

"What the hell happened to you?" he asked, looking over the knight.

His chest heaving as his strength failed, Tristan pawed at his jumper and realised it was covered in blood and whatever he'd thrown up. Holes appeared in places Eleanor's blood had soaked through, eating away the fabric like it had his throat.

"The Unhallowed," he wheezed.

Nye knelt before him, his face coming into focus. "Are you all right?"

He nodded and curled his hand around his throat. "Her blood was like acid."

"What's going on?"

Tristan froze at the sound of Isobel's voice at the door, and he stared up at her. He couldn't take his eyes off the human girl.

"Isobel," Nye said, frowning at Tristan's reaction. "Go to the kitchen and get some blood from the fridge."

She stared at the knight a moment longer, then nodded. "Sure."

When she was gone, he managed to pull his gaze away. "I got away," he said. "She lured me into a trap."

"She?" Nye asked. "Did she say who she was? Were there others?"

He swallowed hard. "Yes. There are others..."

Isobel appeared again, and he hesitated as Nye

took the blood bags from her trembling fingers. She was a good person. She wanted to help them so desperately but was helpless. Maybe there was a way she could help...

Nye handed him the blood and helped him into the armchair. Ripping off the tab at the top of the first bag, he sucked greedily, the blood soothing the razor blades in his throat and stomach.

"Will he be okay?" Isobel asked Nye, watching as the knight devoured the blood without a care for what he looked like.

"He will," the spy replied. "Go back to your room."

Isobel hesitated and then slowly backed out of the study, leaving the two vampires alone.

Tristan drank the last of the blood, the burning sensation finally subsiding to a simmer that was already beginning to fade as his body healed itself.

"You want to tell me what happened?"

He glanced at Nye and nodded. "Eleanor."

Nye visibly stiffened. "What?"

"She's alive," he replied. "I don't know how, but she attacked me. Held me down and tried to turn me into one of her corpses."

"Eleanor is responsible for the..." Nye let his head fall into his hands. "How is this possible?"

"I don't think she's workin' alone," Tristan went on. "She seemed to allude to others."

"*How is she alive?*" Nye roared, tightening his hands

into fists. "*I cut off that bitch's head four hundred years ago!*"

"How the hell should I know? I saw her. She was flesh and blood…" His fingers rose to touch his throat. "I bit her… Her blood was like acid."

"A bitch with acid in her veins," Nye drawled. "Sounds about right. What did she want? To kill you?"

"I don't know. She didn't get very far before I got away." He pulled up his jumper, but his skin had healed. "She was carvin' somethin' but it's gone now."

"Good. Last thing we need is you turning into a walking corpse."

"There's somethin' in this house they want desperately," he said, glancing at Nye.

"I think I already get that, but thanks for the refresher."

Tristan's mind was foggy, details of his encounter with Eleanor scrambled in his mind. "I don't think they just want to kill you…"

Nye rolled his eyes. "No, they want to torture me for their own amusement before they rip me apart."

"I think you should summon Gabby," Tristan said. "This is outside of my knowledge…"

"After a week and half?" Nye scoffed. "No. I can handle this on my own. Eleanor is my problem."

"Her blood was acid, Nye. I don't think she's a witch anymore."

"Not a witch?" he replied, his eyebrows rising. "Then what is she?"

Tristan shook his head slowly, his senses starting to return. "I don't know, but we need to find out. I'm a thousand years old, so she shouldn't have been able to subdue me as easily as she did."

"Maybe you have a point." Nye rose to his feet and began pacing in front of the fireplace. On his second turn, he glanced at Tristan.

"Call her, Nye." The spy waved him off, and he shrugged. "*It's your funeral.*"

"You should go get some rest," Nye said finally. "You look like shit."

Rolling his eyes, he replied, "Thanks for the vote of confidence."

Knowing there was nothing else he could say to sway him, Tristan stood and shuffled toward the door. Let him make his own mistakes. There was only so much he could do to convince him. Maybe Isobel could sway him.

As he returned to his room on the other side of the mansion, he made a mental note to talk to her when he felt better.

<hr>

When Tristan was long gone, Nye picked up his phone and opened the contacts.

The knight was right. Seeing him on the floor like that, totally spent from a five-minute encounter with Eleanor, had shaken him...and he hadn't been the one to feel the tip of her blade this time.

Eleanor was alive. How was the even possible? What power could bring back a headless corpse? If what Tristan had seen was real, then the reflection he'd seen in the off-license the night before was real. She'd been there, watching his every move and then some.

Breathing deeply, he could still smell the lingering scent of Isobel in the room. Her appearance moments before was the first he'd seen of her since he'd lost control and... Her blood had been so sweet and pure. Better than any he'd tasted in a very long time. Just the thought of it had his teeth aching, threatening to grow into the fangs that could rip into her flesh.

Closing his eyes, he took a deep breath and closed off all his senses but the one he needed the most. Sucking up his pride, he took Tristan's advice.

Pressing his thumb on the screen where Gabby's name was displayed, he listened as it began to ring and waited until the call connected.

She answered after the fifth tone.

"It's been a week and a half, Nye. You haven't burned all your bridges already, have you?"

"No, don't be ridiculous," he drawled. "And hello to you, too."

"What is it? I've been having a wonderful break from vampire drama. It's refreshing not having to use my powers to battle ancient curses and creatures, you know."

"Good for you."

"Spit it out. I haven't got all night."

"We've got a problem," he said. "A big one."

There was pause on the other end, and then Gabby asked, "What kind of problem?"

"Someone broke a window. And there's a painting hanging in the foyer that's worth ten million pounds."

"Quit it, Nye. I expect this kind of runaround from Zac, not you. Just say what you mean or hang up and leave me alone."

"A coven of witches called the Unhallowed have been planting spells all over the city and murdering vampires. They tried to kill Tristan tonight."

"Tristan? But he's... Is he okay?"

"Yes, he will be, but he said it was close."

"Hell... I'm sorry, Nye. I..."

"Have you heard of them before?" he asked, turning the conversation back to their current problem.

"The Unhallowed? Never heard of them, but there are a lot of covens out there. Some go back to near the beginning of our kind, to those that are first generation. Even covens that span all elemental affinities. There's no way that any one person could follow them all. If things went to plan like they were supposed to, then there was only ever going to be five covens. Now there are thousands... These Unhallowed witches could have been flying under the radar for a long time."

"It doesn't matter if you've heard of them or not," he shot back, not needing the history lesson. "It's what they're doing now that's a thorn in my side."

"Go on..."

He took a deep breath and told her the whole convoluted story, minus the part where Isobel was trapped inside the mansion and the lines had become blurry as hell. Alex would love that, and if he wasn't careful, Gabby was one breath away from telling the newborn vampire all about it.

"I really need your help, Gabby," he said, laying it all out there. "I don't know what else to do."

"Nye Saer putting his city before his pride," the witch replied. "Perhaps we made the right decision, after all."

"Are you going to help or not?" he asked, rolling his eyes.

"It's my house, and London was Regulus's city," she came back with, her voice wavering slightly as she uttered her dead love's name. "It's my home, too. My home that I allow you to live in and direct your kingdom from. I'm not going to let some crazyass witch with a vendetta against her ex-boyfriend stuff it all up."

Nye's lips curved into a smile as some of the tension left his shoulders. "I'll see you tomorrow, then?"

"I'll be on the next flight out."

CHAPTER 11

Gabby rolled her suitcase up the path that threaded through the front garden of the Hampstead mansion.

Her mansion. It still felt weird saying that considering a few months ago, she only had a few hundred dollars in her savings account and a dead-end job at a Realtor's office in a tiny town in backwater Louisiana, USA. Now she was the multi-millionaire heiress to her dead vampire boyfriend's fortune that had been amassed over two thousand years. Try to explain that one to the IRS.

It might've been jet lag after the nightmare flight she'd just gotten off, but she felt the tingle of unfamiliar magic and shivered. Staring up at the house, she narrowed her eyes, and the image shimmered slightly. Yes, something was definitely there, and it wasn't her magic. It made her skin tingle like she had pins and needles all over the longer she tried to feel it out.

Further prodding revealed it to be some kind of barrier, but what for? Gabby could feel the web all around the mansion, its tendrils gripping tight to the facade, closing over windows and doors.

Letting go of her suitcase, she turned around and peered at the garden. She felt it there, too. There were wards around the perimeter of the property, but they were clumsy, like whoever had cast them had been a novice or hadn't really cared. What the hell had Nye been doing while she was away?

Grasping the handle of her suitcase once more, she rolled it up the remainder of the path and stuck her key into the front door. Unlocking it, she dragged her luggage into the foyer.

"Nye!" she yelled, her voice echoing through the cavernous house. "You'd better be here!"

"Gabby?"

At the sound of a familiar voice, she glanced at the stairs where an excited Isobel was galloping down two at a time. She was the last person Gabby was expecting to see, especially since Alex was still in Ashburton.

"Izzy?" she asked, her eyebrows rising in surprise. "What are you doing here?"

Isobel bounded across the foyer and threw her arms around her neck, hugging her tightly. It was a much warmer welcome than Nye would've given her, that's for sure.

"It's so good to see you," Isobel murmured, sounding tired. "I thought I'd never get out of here."

"Get out of here?" Gabby pulled away and frowned. "What do you mean?"

Isobel's expression fell, and she glanced over her shoulder. "He didn't tell you, did he?"

Gabby's eyes narrowed as the pieces began to fall into place. "Tell me what?"

Her friend shuffled nervously, unsure of what to say, and Gabby began to seethe. Of all the stupid things that vampire could do...

"*Nye!*" she screeched, stepping around Isobel and thundering up the stairs.

Shoving into the study, she found Nye perched on top of the desk, waiting for her imminent arrival.

"What is Isobel doing here?" she demanded.

He gazed at her for a moment and shrugged. Something fishy was going on here, and she was going to get it out of the vampire even if she had to make a few of his brain cells pop.

"Seriously? Is that all you've got to say about imprisoning Isobel against her will?"

"If you stop to think about it, you'll understand why," he replied drolly.

"What did you do to her?"

"Excuse me?" he asked, rising to his feet.

"You've done something to her," she declared. "I saw the way you looked at her in Oxford. *We all did.*"

"Are you insinuating that I compelled her to

remain in the mansion as my pet?" His eyes narrowed, and she knew she had at least some of it right.

She crossed her arms over her chest. "Right now, I am."

"She came to see Alex a week and a half ago," he began, and Gabby's mouth fell open. "Things have not been going smoothly in your absence. She was on the doorstep, and by then, it was already too late. If you know anything about vampire politics, you know this. I kept Isobel here to protect her. From the vampires and now from the Unhallowed."

There was so much wrong with this Gabby didn't even know where to start. "The Unhallowed? What have they done to her that you've so conveniently left out?"

"The corpse..." His eyes lowered. "It was stronger than we anticipated and got into the house..."

"*It attacked her?*"

"You must understand, Gabby, I never intended..."

He turned away, obviously feeling guilty over his part in Isobel's predicament. He was right about her being in danger from the London vampires, but not telling Gabby about it before now was madness. There was so much she could've done to prevent much of the chaos that had already fallen into Nye's lap.

Then there was Alex. There was no way she was telling a newborn founding vampire that his human sister was in the crosshairs of a city of vampires and an unknown coven of witches.

Sinking down into Regulus's favourite armchair, she sighed. "Tell me about the Unhallowed."

Nye glanced at her over his shoulder. "Are you sure? You must be tired…"

"*Tell me, Nye.* No more avoiding or leaving out important details. Just give it to me straight."

"The Unhallowed have been attempting to siphon power from their victims. Carving their symbols and runes into the flesh of the dead and bringing them back to life. They did it once, but we stopped them the second time, and then they attempted it with Tristan. *Eleanor* attempted it. It was the same thing she tried to do to me the day I killed her."

"Who's Eleanor?" Gabby asked.

"The witch I thought I loved back in the early sixteenth century," he explained. "She went against her coven to be with me, and when they found out, they turned her against me. She was in the middle of carving my forehead up when Regulus showed."

At the mention of her dead love, Gabby stiffened. "Regulus?"

"It was the day I first met him," Nye said. "He saved me from Eleanor that day and the Unhallowed in the decades after, and in return, I became one of the first members of the Six. Now the Unhallowed are back."

"Not just the Unhallowed," she drawled.

"No, not just them. I don't understand how Eleanor has survived all this time. I cut off her head, and that's a pretty final way of dying. Perhaps it has to do with the siphoning. Aya had her head cut off once, and she's still around…"

"The Unhallowed are siphoning power?" Gabby asked with a frown. It was the second time he'd used that word. "What do you mean by that?"

"They use spells—symbols—to drain someone of their power," he said. "It's what happened to the two vampires we've found so far. The first was reanimated, and the second we don't know because I had it burned to ash by Reed."

"Who's Reed?"

"The leader of the new and improved Six."

Gabby rolled her eyes. "Great."

"They were needed," he replied. "And Reed has been invaluable."

Gabby wasn't listening, not really. Her thoughts were dwelling on the word Nye had used. Siphoning. It meant to take a creature's power and possess it, almost like charging a battery.

"Witches channel another's power like a conduit," she said after a moment. "We don't take it. We can't."

Nye's brow furrowed, and he moved to sit across from her. "So a witch can't siphon?"

"No, not really. It doesn't work like that."

"Sabine is obviously a hack, then," Nye muttered. "She's so fired."

"Who's Sabine?" Gabby asked. "If she's the witch who made that mess in the yard, then yeah, fire her."

He snorted, and she knew there was more to that

story, too. This witch had probably been trying to wrap him around her little finger. Too bad he seemed to be preoccupied with her human friend down the hall. That was another problem, and one she'd deal with once they'd figured out this Unhallowed snake pit.

"There's only one explanation I can think of for this," she mused aloud. "It's so farfetched I've got to be wrong."

"Trust me, farfetched is better than nothing right now. Not when a witch that's supposed to be four hundred years dead in the ground is trying to carve her finger paintings into the chest of my right-hand man."

"Tristan... Has he recovered?" she asked.

"Yes, he seems fine now. I think his pride was hurt a little, though. He's out with the Six looking for signs of Eleanor's graffiti."

"Good, but you should warn him and your little personal guard as soon as possible because if I'm right, there's no fighting this thing. Not by you or them."

Nye leaned forward, resting his elbows on his knees. "What do you think they are, Gabby?"

"Wraiths," she said simply.

"Wraiths?" Nye asked, cocking his head to the side.

"They haven't been seen in hundreds, bordering on thousands, of years. At least, not in any written history I've seen," she explained. "Wraiths siphon power from other witches, vampires, living creatures, even ley lines —the spiritual energy of the earth. They deal in dark, evil magic. If that's the case, then I'm not sure what I can do. I have no idea how to fight something that's not meant to exist anymore. A vampire, even one as old as Tristan, sure as hell doesn't have any power against them."

He snorted and rubbed his eyes, feeling tired, which was difficult for a vampire with boundless energy. "So you're saying we're dealing with immortal, ghostly super witches?"

"The immortal part is sketchy but pretty much."

"There must be a way to get rid of them..."

She shrugged. Just when life was beginning to calm down, in rolled Nye and his ex-girlfriend. It was all a little taxing right after a long-haul flight from America.

Nye waved his hand around, gesturing to the walls filled with grimoires. "You have the wealth of knowledge Regulus collected over thousands of years at your fingertips. I'm sure there's something in one of these musty old books that can help."

It was entirely possible, but she was offended by Nye's flippant tone. It was her house, so she was a part of this mess, no matter how much she wanted out. Anyway, she might be the only one who had a chance of unraveling whatever the Unhallowed had put into motion.

"I'd like to talk with Tristan when he gets back," she said, ignoring the spy. "I want to make sure he's all right."

"I'll let him know." He glanced toward the place Gabby knew Isobel's room was. "Is there anything you can do about the wards in the yard? The mansion should be fortified.”

“Yes, I know a few that should do the trick.” She narrowed her eyes, her thoughts going to her friend. Nye was awfully interested in her well-being, and she was beginning to think there was more to it than just crossing Alex.

“Nye...what exactly is going on with you and Isobel?”

“Do the wards cover wraiths?” he asked, ignoring her question.

“The spell extends to wraiths,” she replied with a sigh, knowing she wouldn’t get it out of him anytime soon. Isobel on the other hand... “Don’t worry about that. Isobel will be safe inside the house. I’ll recast all the wards in the garden as a precaution, but it’ll take some time.”

“What about the barrier on the house?”

“I can’t remove it without a great deal of hassle,” she replied. “I think it’s best to leave it intact for now. That’s the one thing this Sabine did well.”

He nodded. “What can I do now?”

“For starters, you can go get my suitcase from the foyer and bring it to my room. I’m going to see Izzy and get her side of the story.”

Nye’s eyes widened, and he began to open his mouth to complain, but she was already on her feet and at the study door. She was not beholden to comply with his commands. He was the leader of the London *vampires*, not witches, and Gabby was a witch unto her own, anyway. She had no coven or duty to adhere to other than her own conscience. In many ways, it was a blessing to have the freedom she did even though she felt lonely on occasion.

Nye had given Isobel the room at the end of the hall. Gabby knocked softly on the door and then opened it a crack. Izzy was sitting on the couch, her hopeful gaze fixed on the door. Sliding through the gap, Gabby smiled at her friend.

"He gave you the best room in the house," she mused, glancing around the posh interior. King-sized bed, separate sitting area with a couch and matching armchairs, massive television, walk-in robe, and a black marble bathroom with an epic tub. Pretty swish. The view over the back garden was pretty up there as well.

"Oh?" Izzy asked, glancing around.

"I took Regulus's old room," she went on, beginning to realise Izzy meant more to Nye than just a passing flirtation. "It's on the other side of the mansion, but this is pretty nice."

She stood there for a moment, regarding their predicament. It felt a little strange to see Isobel here in the mansion, and when Alex found out she'd been dragged into one of their supernatural messes, he'd be livid. Best to keep him in the dark until the moment they couldn't put it off any longer.

"It's really great to see you, Gabby," Isobel said, her

shoulders sinking. "I was beginning to think I was alone in here."

"You're never alone, Izzy," she replied, sitting beside her on the couch.

She attempted a smile, but it faded as soon as it appeared.

"How are you?" she asked her friend. "Has Nye been treating you okay? Did they remember to feed you?"

Isobel laughed. "Getting fed was an experience. Have you seen the contents of your fridge?"

"*Have I ever.*"

They sat in silence for a moment, the weight of all the crazy things that had happened hanging over their heads.

"What exactly happened to get you stuck in here?" Gabby asked after a moment. "Nye likes to spin his own stories, so I'd like to hear it from you."

"What's there to tell?" she replied. "I came looking for Alex. I hadn't heard from him since he left Oxford, and it wasn't until I was here that Nye told me he'd gone home with you. Apparently, by then, it was too late to avoid being stuck here. Nye lured me inside like a creepy kidnapper with a lollypop."

"Is that all?" she asked, but Isobel wasn't listening.

"You can talk to him," she said, taking Gabby's hands. "You can convince him to let me go home."

"Uh..." she began, and Isobel shook her head.

"I'm stuck here like a useless lump," she argued.

"He won't let me help, he won't explain everything, he won't talk to me after he…" She pulled her hands away and shook her head in frustration.

"After he what?"

"It doesn't even matter," she said, her voice wavering. "His silence is all the answer I need."

"Isobel," Gabby prodded. "What did Nye do to you?"

"Nothing I didn't want to happen," she replied sheepishly. "Well, except for the…*thing*."

"Thing?"

"We were, uh…" She gestured to the couch they sat on. "And he, uh…"

Gabby almost leapt off the couch. "You were *making out* with him?"

"He got a little carried away," Isobel said, trying to calm her. "He warned me, and I pushed him too far…"

"*He bit you?*" Gabby exclaimed, finally allowing her mind to slot the pieces together.

"Tristan healed me," Isobel went on like she was making an excuse for the spy. "But ever since, it's been like he's a ghost. I saw him once when Tristan was attacked… Or at least, I think he was attacked since nobody will tell me what's going on."

Gabby couldn't get over the fact that Nye had ripped into her friend's skin and fed from her. Not by a long shot. "I'm going to wring his filthy—"

"How's Alex?" Izzy asked, looking hopeful. "I'm

worried about him. His life is all screwed up, and he went home to... *I can't even say it.*"

"Alex is handling things pretty well," Gabby said, letting her anger simmer down. "He signed over his business to Freddy Hanson."

"Freddy Hanson? The guy he used to work with?"

"The one and the same."

"Good choice."

"He's okay, Izzy. The first few months are going to be tough, but he'll get through it. He's got you."

Isobel rolled her eyes. "Fat lot of good I'll do. I try to understand all this vampire stuff, but I'm just clueless. It's not like there's a handbook anywhere I can study. I'm a gun at research and analysis. I try to listen to things around here, but they're vampires with super hearing and know how to talk at levels only dogs can hear."

Gabby stifled a laugh. It must have been really colourful around here with Isobel on deck to hand Nye his ass.

"How much do you know about what's going on around here?" she asked, finally able to settle down from the shock of finding out that Isobel was kissing and dry humping Nye to the point he decided feeding on her was a good idea. It was yet another thing she had to scold the vampire over.

"He told me about the Unhallowed and how they're mad at him for killing one of them like a gazillion years ago. But it took almost getting my face eaten off by a zombie for him to tell me anything," Isobel practically wailed. "I feel so *useless*."

Knowing Izzy, she wouldn't have made it easy for Nye, not for one second. Two strong-minded individuals like those pair were bound to be at each other's throats. Perhaps that was a bad turn of phrase considering the spy's slip.

"So you know about Eleanor," she said.

"Who's Eleanor?" Isobel asked with a frown.

So Nye had left out the part about his ex-lover, then. Perhaps he did care a little about Isobel after all if he was trying to shield her from his past mistakes rather than just compel her to bug off.

"She's one of the Unhallowed witches, apparently," she replied quickly. "We have a name now at least, so it's only a matter of time before we find them and put an end to this crazy revenge plot."

"Is there anything I can do? Do you need a research assistant? Sparring partner? *Anything?*"

"Don't worry too much," Gabby said, knowing Isobel was going stir-crazy locked inside the mansion with all the pent-up sexual tension she had with Nye. "Now that I'm back, I can do my best to bail Nye's ass out of trouble, and you'll be safe to go back to Oxford. I've got your back, Izzy."

Isobel sank back onto the couch with a relieved sigh. "Everything's so screwed up."

Gabby snorted at the irony. "That's just another day in paradise around here."

The air was icy against Nye's skin as he stood in the middle of the woods, flakes of snow sticking to his black woollen coat. His breath plumed out in front of him as he turned, trying to remember where he was, but he couldn't recall.

How did he get here?

Glancing at his feet, he stilled. The snow lay thick on the ground, stained red with a torrent of blood, but no body was anywhere to be seen. He was alone...or was he?

The hairs on the back of his neck began to tingle and he turned, his gaze meeting a familiar one. *Eleanor*.

Her hair was out, strands of wild curls haloing her pale features, and her cheeks flushed pink in the cold air. He saw her long skirts and cloak and remembered it was what she was wearing the day she died. This whole place...it was where he'd killed her.

"I find it curious how even the immortal never stray

too far from where they were born," she said, her voice loud in the silence. "No matter what they've become."

"What is this?" he asked, looking around at the snow-covered clearing.

"It's just a dream," she replied, laying a hand over his heart. "Don't look so panicked."

"Vampires don't dream," he snapped, pushing her away.

Eleanor smiled and drew her hand under her cloak. "Are you afraid?"

Nye narrowed his eyes and snorted. "Not of you."

"Ah, perhaps not, but you are afraid of something, dear Nye. What could it be?" She moved silently over the snow, circling him as she pondered her own question.

Her boots made no sound as she walked. The air was still, and the animals of the woods were nowhere to be found. If she was trying to trick him with this glimpse of his past, she certainly lacked the attention to detail that it required.

"You're wasting your time, Eleanor," he said. "You will fail, just as you did the first time."

She laughed softly. "You're still the same as I remember you. Passionate yet arrogant. Handsome and naive... You think all this is about you?" Her laughter grew. "Oh, dear Nye. You poor lost little boy."

"Then what is it about?"

She stopped in front of him, and her smile faded. "*Me.*"

One moment, Nye was standing there letting her declaration sink in, and the next, he was flying across the clearing, his limbs flapping uselessly. His body collided with a tree, his head cracking against the trunk.

Eleanor stood before him, her body melding against his as her arms wrapped around his neck like a lover. Just as she had the day she'd attacked him outside of York.

"It's only a matter of time," she purred, and the vision dissolved, melting into nothingness.

Gasping for air, Nye sat up in bed, his chest heaving.

Darkness surrounded him, his bedroom empty save for his sorry ass.

Rubbing his mouth, he realised his fangs were bared, ready to rip Eleanor's throat out...but she'd just been in his dream. She wasn't real...or was she? He wouldn't put it past the Unhallowed to put visions in his mind to unsettle his nerves and corrode his strength. Or perhaps it was his own mind bringing his fears to life.

Climbing out of bed, he padded into the bathroom and splashed water on his face, clearing the remnants of sleep from his eyes. Staring at his reflection, he studied the rise and fall of his scar, the memory of steel slicing into his flesh rising from the darkness. Fire, screams, blood, and another kind of kiss. Salt searing into his human flesh as he sank beneath the waves of the burning ocean, the tide ebbing and flowing, sucking him deeper toward death.

What kind of life would Isobel have had if he'd drowned in the ocean that night as the Spanish Armada burned atop the heaving English Channel?

Hissing, he turned, strode into the bedroom, and pulled on a shirt and a pair of trousers. There was no way he was resting easy tonight.

<hr>

Nye found himself in the foyer of the mansion.

He stood before the painting Isobel told him was worth a great deal of money. A lost relic of the Renaissance, and here it was, hanging in Regulus's house, the Roman having no regard for its place in human history. Perhaps it was a metaphor for their kind and their inability to care about mortality. Or maybe he'd just liked the painting.

What had Isobel called it? He didn't remember because he'd been too busy watching her rather than listening. Eleanor was right. He wasn't afraid of the Unhallowed coming to kill him. He was afraid of something else. Something more profound.

"Nye, what are you doin'?"

He glanced over his shoulder at the appearance of Tristan and wished the knight would just go away and leave him be, but he knew he wasn't getting out of this without a grilling.

"What are you doing here, more like it," he replied. "It's three in the morning."

"I've just returned from my evenin' scavenger hunt," the knight replied.

"Find anything?"

"Nothin'. It's quiet out there." Tristan stood beside him and stared at the painting. "A little too quiet if you ask me. The vampires seemed to have settled for the time bein'. There haven't been any more symbols or corpses, either."

"A moment of reprieve, then."

"Perhaps they sense Gabby has returned and are waitin' to see what you do to combat the Unhallowed threat."

"Perhaps..." Nye muttered, his mind still hazy from his earlier vision. *It was only a matter of time.* Until what?

"How is Isobel?" Tristan asked after a moment.

He shrugged. That was a can of worms he'd stayed right away from. After biting her like he had—hell, it was unforgivable despite his constant warnings—the temptation had been too strong. His attraction to her overwhelming from the moment her lips had touched his. There was only one way the interlude could have ended—no matter how hard he'd tried to fight it. Nature had won out, and ever since, Nye had avoided her like the plague.

Tristan turned to face him. "You haven't been to see her since—"

"Don't you even say it, Tristan," he spat.

The knight shrugged. "If you feel that strongly about her, then you should apologise. She had a great deal of questions when I went to heal her."

Nye scowled, turning his attention back to the painting. The thought of Tristan putting his filthy hands on Isobel to heal her when he should've been strong enough to do it himself, made his blood boil.

He and Tristan had almost become friends over the past months—ever since they'd united against Aed —but his helping Nye with the London vampires didn't replace two hundred years of loathing overnight. The vampire's constant observations about his feelings for Isobel weren't doing much to cement goodwill, either.

"She's tryin' to understand," Tristan continued. "I can tell her whatever she wants to know about our kind, but it's not me she wants to hear it from."

"The less she knows about this world, the better."

"Do you really believe that? With what her brother has become?"

"I have to believe in something. This belief will save Isobel from certain death, and I get to keep my head when Alex returns."

"If you need to believe in somethin', believe in her strength. Death is not certain on either path."

"She needs to live a normal life," he said thinly. "Remaining here, when this is all said and done, will only put her in more danger. Isn't that love, Tristan?

Protecting someone we care about even at the expense of our own feelings?"

"Yes...and no." The knight frowned and shook his head. "We've all done things we aren't proud of, Nye, but it doesn't mean you should deny yourself happiness if you have the chance. Things that are unforgivable to us are forgivable to others. That is where we find our redemption."

"A human cannot survive in this world," Nye declared stubbornly.

Tristan smiled and looked the spy over. "Perhaps not on their own."

"Over a thousand years old and you're still a romantic. I'm beginning to believe you were dropped on your head as a child."

"*The night is dark and full of terrors*," Tristan quoted, ignoring his comment. "*But the fire burns them all away.*"

Nye snorted, recognising the line from Tristan's favourite television program. "You have a problem."

The knight laughed and walked away. "Me and a billion other people on this earth."

Nye turned back to the painting once more and studied the lines and swashes of paint that only his vampire eyes could see. Tristan had a peculiar way of getting his point across, but the more he thought about it, the more he realised he had to make a decision. Let Isobel go or...

Be the fire.

CHAPTER 13

Isobel stared out the kitchen windows at the darkening world beyond and sighed.

The hues of orange and yellow that lit up the sky were brilliant tonight. The brief English summer was well and truly underway. She could open a window and let the breeze and scent of the garden flow inside, but she couldn't go out among it.

She didn't realise how much she missed sitting outside her favourite pub in Oxford with her friends from the University Masters program until she wasn't able. Funny how life worked.

Then there was Nye. Nye, who kissed her like he was starving for affection. Nye, who wanted it from *her*. Nye, who had all but disappeared without a trace. She knew he was around because she'd heard him talking to Gabby, but not once had she seen his face outside of the incident with Tristan. Even then, she'd been dismissed like an annoying little fly.

Isobel knew she didn't belong, but she sure as hell didn't need the constant reminder.

"Good evenin', Isobel."

She turned as Tristan appeared behind her, a smile on his face. At least someone around here was happy.

"Tristan," she said. "I didn't see you there."

He came to stand beside her, his gaze following hers. "The sunset used to be the sweetest moment of the day," he mused. "Back when I was first turned. It was when I was finally able to go outside and breathe clearly."

She'd never known Tristan to talk about his early life as a vampire, but then again, she didn't really know him that well. There were a great deal of questions she wanted to ask the knight, and not all of them had to do with his nature. All the history that was available to humanity was limited to what scribes had deigned to write down. Tristan had actually lived through a thousand years of it. He'd marched with the Knights Templar on the Crusades, and that in itself was a wealth of knowledge she was dying to tap into.

However, she was currently living in a world she didn't understand. There was no handbook or guide to tell her how things worked or how to act. She could watch all the television she wanted, but it was just fiction.

"How can you go out into the sunlight?" she asked, trying to make an effort. "I know it has to do with magic, but I don't quite understand."

His lips curved into a smile, and he inclined his head. "Some vampires have an item of jewellery that contains a spell to block the effects of the sun. They have to wear it always. Otherwise, they would burn. Others have a spell that is weaved into their very bein'. It's a more permanent solution, though it can be removed."

"Their body is spelled like the barrier on the house?" she asked.

"Somethin' like that. It requires a powerful witch to be able to weave that kind of web. Not all vampires are lucky enough to find someone who is willin' to cast a spell that complicated."

"Do you have a...web?"

"Yes."

Isobel glanced back at the yard beyond the windows.

"Are you feelin' better now that Gabby has returned?" Tristan asked.

"A little, though she's busy helping Nye with the Unhallowed, I guess."

"You must miss goin' outside," he said after a moment. "Maybe we can ask Gabby if the barrier can extend out onto the patio."

Isobel thought that sounded heavenly, but she still hesitated. "Wouldn't it leave me exposed? Vampires can't come in the house, but out there..."

"Gabby has cast wards around the grounds," he

explained. "We would know if anythin' is comin' long before it was a problem."

"Maybe..." she said uncertainly. "It would be nice to go out into the sunshine for a while. The weather has been really good."

"I'll ask her if it's a possibility."

She smiled despite the air of melancholy she'd been carrying around since 'the incident' with Nye. "That would be nice."

Tristan nodded. "I'll put it to her." He glanced outside again and said, "I have some business to attend to. Do you need anythin'?"

Isobel shook her head and ran her hands up and down her arms as they began to prickle with goose bumps. There was a sudden chill on the air that had her shivering as she watched Tristan cross the patio and disappear into the yard. Ironically, she didn't feel any better than when he'd first appeared.

Sighing, she turned to the kitchen and began pulling food out from the fridge to start cooking for her dinner. It still flipped her out when she opened the door and saw all the blood hanging around next to the pint of milk. It was yet another reminder of her predicament.

Dinner was a lonely affair, being the only one present in the gigantic house, and she was dwarfed by the size of the island bench with her single plate, single knife, and single fork. It was all a little depressing.

Isobel didn't know what made her stand up, walk across the kitchen, and open the back door, but she turned the handle and tugged. Breathing deeply, her eyes widened as the heady scent of the garden beyond filled her nose. It was all flowers and grass with a hint of sunshine that had lingered from that afternoon. She'd never paid much attention to these things before, but after being stuck in the mansion for two weeks, her nose must have developed a sensitivity for all things outside. It was heaven.

Impulsively, she lifted her hand and went to press it against the barrier. The last time she'd tried to beat her way through it, her skin had tingled when it came into contact with the magic. It had reminded her of an electric fence giving her a warning zap. Still, what was the harm?

Pressing her hand against the opening, she stumbled slightly when it went straight through.

The barrier was gone.

Maybe Tristan had been super efficient and had come through on his word. Gabby must've shaped the limits of the magic to the patio, but she still felt uneasy even considering going against Nye's wishes. Nye, who hadn't said more than two words to her since they'd shared that unbelievably passionate kiss. Yeah, he'd sunk his fangs into her neck and she'd stabbed him with a pen, but her feeble human mind had held onto the part where he'd wanted her. Not for dinner but romantically.

Ever since, she had wondered if she'd dreamed the conversations she'd had with him for all the care and affection he'd shown her. She was beginning to think he saw touching her as a mistake. Everything about the last two weeks had been the biggest stuff up of them all.

She didn't belong here, and her humanity had seen to that. She couldn't help, she couldn't leave, and she couldn't even fight to save herself from that zombie. She felt useless and nothing but a burden. She didn't belong, and Nye's absence in the wake of such passion had done nothing but cement it.

Isobel knew she was tempting fate, but she was so starved for human interaction and acceptance she stepped outside.

Instantly, she felt the breeze on her face and closed her eyes, tilting her chin up to the sky, imagining the sun was beating down onto her pale skin. The moon would have to do for now, but it still felt glorious.

The mansion was her prison, and the city outside was her salvation. Out here, she could find a place where someone wanted her instead of merely tolerating her presence. Out here, she was free.

Squashing down the little voice in the back of her mind telling her to go back inside, she walked forward, putting one foot in front of the other. She ventured further out into the garden, testing the new limits of her world.

Isobel found herself at the bottom of the garden

before she realised. Standing underneath the impressive olive tree she'd admired from her bedroom window, she stared at the plaque at the base of the trunk and gasped.

Regulus was buried underneath it. Like, *right there*. Why hadn't anyone mentioned it? Even as the thought left her head, she knew the answer. No one had cared to tell her much of anything, so why should she be surprised.

An overwhelming surge of loneliness welled up inside her, and she swallowed a sob that had risen in her throat. She didn't know what to do anymore. Her life was a total shambles. She'd missed two weeks of classes and appointments with her thesis advisor, and there was no way she was catching up now. She'd tried to keep studying, but she needed to be in Oxford at the University library. If she wasn't wanted, then why couldn't she just go home? Really, what did she have to go back to now, anyway?

She pulled in a shaky breath and stared down at the ground where Regulus was buried. She bet he didn't have this kind of problem. He'd probably just taken whatever he wanted because he was an immortal asshole.

"Isobel?"

Gasping, she turned on her heel and stumbled against the trunk of the olive tree as her gaze collided with an unknown woman. She was lingering in the darkness like a creeper, a hoodie pulled up over her head. Even in the dark, Isobel could see the woman's hair was long and wild, the hood hardly containing the mess of curls. She was tiny, but there was something about her she couldn't quite put her finger on.

"Who are you?" she asked, giving her the once-over. Damn, the stranger was supermodel thin in her skinny jeans and had the thigh gap going on and everything.

"I'm Eleanor," the woman declared, removing her hood.

Isobel stepped backward, her heart beginning to pound. If she was the Unhallowed witch who was responsible for all the carnage, then she was in real trouble.

"I don't want to hurt you," she said, holding up her hands. "I just wanted the chance to talk to you."

"Talk to me?" Isobel asked. "Why on earth do I matter? I'm just a human."

She smiled. "Because Nye loves you."

She drew in a shaky breath and stared the witch down. If she was trying to intimidate the poor little human, she was in for a rude awakening. "That may be the case," she said. "And if he does, then what's stopping you from using me to get to him? *Nothing*. Then just do what you're going to do, Eleanor. I know I have no chance in hell of going up against you and winning. I'm just a plain human with nothing but my sharp wit to protect myself with."

Eleanor smiled widely and laughed. "I can see it

now. What he sees in you. It was the same thing he saw in me."

She frowned and really wished she had the foresight to bring a knife with her from the kitchen. "What are you talking about?"

"Didn't he tell you? We were in love once...until he cut off my head. It's a cruel way to break it off with a woman, don't you think?"

"He... He..." She was a fool to think he'd never been with another woman before, but Eleanor? He'd *loved* her? It was totally irrational, but she felt a hot spike of jealousy stab right through her heart. Why did she even care anymore? Nye didn't even want her for *her*. He sure loved sucking on her neck but had dropped her the moment he realised what he'd done. She was Alex's sister, and apparently, that made her off limits.

Eleanor stepped closer. "He hasn't told you the whole story, Isobel. What is love without truth?"

Yeah, what was love without truth? There hadn't been much of that since the day she'd arrived.

"Come," the witch said, taking her hand. "We have much to discuss."

"Well, that was a bust," Gabby declared as she stood beside Nye on the footpath. "It's like these people don't even exist."

Nye had accompanied Gabby as she followed a lead on the Unhallowed. Apparently, the witch who ran the occult shop in this posh little corner of London was something of a witchy almanac. That was short for she was a know-it-all. Being a vampire, Nye was forced to wait outside like a commoner with no regard for who he was...which was the leader of the London vampires, *and don't you forget it.*

"So she wasn't as smart as she claimed," he drawled, glaring at the shop window full of crystals, dream catchers, and cheap dragon statues. The moment the door had opened, the stink of incense had almost made him retch.

"She's smarter than you," Gabby retorted, glaring at him. "But we're talking about witches who have somehow turned themselves into wraiths."

"Supposedly," he interjected.

"*Supposedly*," she snapped. "Either way, we're talking about something that hasn't existed for a thousand years. Knowledge can fade to myth and then to nothing given enough time." She turned on her heel and began walking away.

Nye fell into step beside her, sulking over many things, including their lack of a lead against the Unhallowed, but what he'd done to Isobel bothered him most of all.

Stopping beside a sleek, black car, Gabby wrenched open the back door before the driver had a chance to get out and open it for her. Sliding inside, Nye sighed and reluctantly followed.

Now that Gabby was home, the driver and the car had been put back into use. It was one of Regulus's vices that hadn't quite carried over to him. It belonged to the witch, along with everything else the Roman had accumulated in his two thousand years. Nye had never thought it important to grow wealth, so he didn't feel the need to use hers to get to where he was going. Literally.

Gabby buried her nose in her grimoire the entire trip back to the mansion, leaving him to stew in his own juices. Eleanor projecting herself into his lack of dreams was creepy enough, but what Tristan had suggested to him pissed him off even more. Talking to him like a relationship counsellor. Like the knight would know shit about love. He'd been pining over Aya for a thousand years, and she'd fallen for Zac and left her companion out to dry. Why should he take Tristan's advice? It was obviously flawed.

Climbing out the car as it came to a stop, he held the door open for Gabby and allowed her to walk ahead. He would have to clear the air with Isobel sooner or later. Perhaps he should explain a few things to her this evening while Gabby continued her search. He should explain to the human girl why it was a terrible idea to allow herself to love a monster like him.

"Nye!"

His head snapped up at the sound of Gabby's

panicked cry. The witch was standing by the front door, staring into the house, and his dead heart stopped beating for a sickening moment.

Something was wrong. Something was *very* wrong.

"The barrier is gone," Gabby said, stepping into the house.

Nye shot forward and grasped her arm. "*Wait.*"

He stepped into the house, listening with everything he had, but only silence greeted him. Isobel's scent was everywhere, dangling in front of him like a carrot, but the house felt eerily empty. Turning to glance out into the night, he knew in his heart she'd left.

This wasn't a coincidence. The Unhallowed must've killed Sabine. *Shit.*

"She's gone," he said, staring toward the street.

"But you haven't looked..."

"I don't need to." He went to step forward, but Gabby put a hand on his chest.

"I'm coming with you."

"No. Stay here, and check the house. Make sure nothing else has been tampered with."

Gabby narrowed her eyes but didn't argue. "Okay."

"I'll find her," he said, more to appease himself than the witch.

Breathing deeply, he walked through the house and into the kitchen. The remains of Isobel's dinner were still on the island bench and had been for some time. Glancing at the open back door, he stepped outside. Here, her presence was everywhere. He felt her lingering against his skin, pulling him forward into the garden, and he allowed his body to act on his behalf, pushing away all rational thought and allowing his vampire senses to lead him.

Nye followed her scent like a bloodhound—which was an ironic metaphor considering the word blood.

He lingered at the bottom of the garden underneath Regulus's olive tree, feeling out the direction she'd gone. The air was so still her scent lingered, mapping out a trail for him to follow like a treasure map.

Practically running through the streets surrounding the mansion, he found himself on the edge of Hampstead Heath, the largest green area within the city limits. It was here the trail evaporated, her scent overwhelmed by nature. Nye didn't care. He'd search all night and the rest of forever until he found her.

Traveling the paths of the Heath, he searched every inch until he came to the southeast corner, and there in the shadow of Kenwood House, he found her.

She sat alone on the shore of the pond, her shoulders slumped, and he was beside her in an instant. Behind them, the lights of London burned in the darkness, the city stretching out toward the horizon.

"Isobel," he said in relief, but she didn't move.

Kneeling beside her, Nye cupped her face and

tilted her chin up. When their gazes met, he frowned. Her eyes were glassy and vacant, the fire he'd come to know completely gone.

"Isobel," he said again, beginning to panic. "Isobel, it's Nye."

She blinked a few times and began to rouse. Her eyes flickered around wildly, confusion clear in her pretty features. "How... How... Where am I?"

"You're in the park near the mansion," he murmured, running his thumb across her flushed cheek. "Hampstead Heath."

"But I... I don't remember..."

"Don't worry about it now," he murmured. "I've found you."

"I'm sorry," she said, her eyes drooping. "I just wanted to go outside."

A twist of pain burst through his heart. He'd forced this on her. He hadn't meant to, but he now understood that she'd been angry, hurt, and alone. That had driven her to leave the first moment she'd had a chance. All she wanted was to belong, and all he'd shown her was how she *didn't*, even though he wanted her affection most of all.

"I'm sorry," he murmured, pulling her against his chest. It felt good to hold her fragile body against his.

Isobel sighed, her breath tickling his neck. "I'm so tired..."

Scooping her up into his arms, Nye carried her

though the Heath, along the darkened streets, and back to the safety of the mansion.

"It's okay," he whispered against the top of her head as he walked. "I've got you."

It was decided. He was going to be the fire.

CHAPTER 14

When the front door burst open with a bang, Gabby was at the top of the stairs in an instant, ready to unleash hell. The house hadn't been disturbed other than the absence of the barrier and Izzy's absence, and she'd been left to wait for Nye to return. So far, there hadn't been any news…until what sounded like an explosion of splitting wood downstairs.

The moment she saw Nye standing in the foyer with a limp Isobel in his arms, she feared the worst. He strode toward her, a look of panic on his face.

"She's not well," he said as he brushed past her.

Gabby frowned and followed the vampire's flight down the hall to Isobel's bedroom.

"Nye, wait," she called out after him, but he wasn't listening.

She lingered in the doorway as he laid Isobel gently on the bed and removed her boots, tossing them onto the floor. He cupped her face while Gabby stood by, but her friend had fallen into a deep sleep, and nothing seemed to rouse her.

"She's..." he began, smoothing her hair behind her ear. "She said she was tired. I could feel it when I found her. She was confused and didn't know where she was or how she'd gotten there..." He swallowed hard, unable to take his eyes from her. "They did something to her. Eleanor did something to her. *I know it.*"

Gabby stepped forward and placed her hand on his shoulder. "Let me see," she murmured.

Nye stood, his shoulders stiff, and allowed her to move into his place. She sat on the bed and took Izzy's hand in her own as she closed her eyes. This was her forte—soul magic—and she excelled in it more than she did any of the other elements. The ether was her blood right, and with it came an affinity for everything the earth had to offer—air, fire, water, and the earth itself. Gabby was blessed with a heavy burden like other witches of her bloodline, but after all the things she'd seen, she wouldn't have it any other way.

Letting her power seep through her skin and into her friend's, she began mapping out the source of energy she'd felt around her. Immediately, Gabby felt the presence of something dark and twisted...with hooked claws and vine-like tendrils crawling all around Izzy's spirit. It was a curse. Someone had lured Isobel from the house and placed a nasty spell deep within the most private parts of a human's essence. It was malicious and cold, and only one person would have been responsible.

Eleanor.

The dark tendrils had snaked through Izzy's flesh and had begun worming their way into her spirit. The longer Gabby let her magic brush against the essence that made her friend who she was, the more she could see the poison.

Opening her eyes, Gabby dropped Isobel's hand. Standing, she pulled up the blankets and tucked her in, aware that Nye was lingering behind her, his anxiety growing. She'd known the vampire had a soft spot for Isobel, and he hadn't tried to hide it when she forced it out of him the other day, but right now, it was looking a lot more serious than she first realised.

"Is she... Will she be all right?" he asked.

"She needs rest," Gabby said, placing a hand on his shoulder in a lame attempt to reassure him.

"She was so tired..." he began. "It was like all the energy had been..." He glanced at Gabby, and she could see the dread in his eyes. "Did they try to siphon from her? Is that what this is?"

Gabby shook her head gently. "No. It's not like that."

"Then what is it? Something isn't right."

She nodded toward the door and nudged his shoulder gently. "Let's talk in the study."

He didn't fight her. He just followed her into the

other room and sank down into one of the armchairs by the fireplace. He looked utterly exhausted, as if the weight on his shoulders had finally broken him.

Closing the door behind her, she sat across from the vampire. "She's been cursed," she said gently.

"What?"

"I can feel it all around her, leeching into her spirit. That's why she's so tired."

"What does that mean? Can't you stop it?"

"The curse is feeding on her strength and strangling her spirit," she explained. "Eventually, she'll fall into a coma and waste away to nothing."

"*No!*" he cried. "That can't happen. *I won't let it.*"

"Do you love her?" she asked, wanting to hear the truth from his lips.

"What?" He stared at her like she was stark raving mad.

"Do you love her, Nye?" she asked more forcibly.

"What—"

"*Answer the question.*"

He rose to his feet and began to shake, his hands curled into tight fists making his knuckles turn white. "Yes. *I can't help it.*"

"That sounds familiar," Gabby said wryly, thinking of how her feelings had exploded all over the place with Regulus. She'd hated him for the things he'd done to her friends and the seemingly unforgivable threats he'd made against her, but despite it all, love had won in the face of adversity.

She was certain the same would happen with Nye and Isobel.

"I'm going to rip Eleanor apart," he snarled. "Cutting off that bitch's head was nothing compared to what I'll do to her now."

"Nye," she declared. "If you go now, you'll be giving the Unhallowed exactly what they want. Stay. When Isobel wakes, she'll need you. Let me work out a way to save you both before you run off and try to play hero. *Please*."

"If I kill her, then Isobel will be cured," he argued. "I've seen it before."

"It doesn't work that way. Once a curse has been placed, killing the witch who cast it won't do a thing. It's not a normal spell, Nye."

He stared at her, a look of pure anguish on his face. "*No...*"

"*I'm sorry*. I wish it was that simple."

He collapsed into the armchair and covered his face with both hands. "Oh God, what have I done?"

"It's not your fault."

"Every part of this is my fault," he snapped, letting his hands fall away. "I locked her up in here against her will, I pushed her away, *I bit her*, and then I did nothing to redeem myself. I allowed her to feel isolated and abandoned when all I wanted to do was—" He stopped himself mid-sentence, his eyes beginning to swirl into the darkness that took all vampires when they became angry enough.

"Blaming yourself isn't going to help anyone, least of all Isobel," Gabby said. "Calm yourself, and go be with her. There's nothing you can help me with for the time being. Let me find a way to unravel the curse, but don't leave Izzy alone."

Nye turned away from her and took a few deep breaths. After a moment, he glided from the room without so much as a word and left her alone.

One thing was glaringly obvious. The Unhallowed had been unsuccessful in all their attempts to get at Nye, so they'd struck where it would hurt the most. By cursing Isobel, Eleanor was banking on Nye going to her. His life for Isobel's, and by the way he'd reacted it was almost a certainty it would happen...unless Gabby could find a way to stop the curse before it ever became a problem.

Then there were the ramifications for Izzy, which she'd conveniently left out of her conversation with Nye. If she couldn't find a way to remove the curse, there was no way of telling what Isobel would become...if she lived long enough to tell the story.

Anything could trigger the spy into doing something rash, especially in his current state. Love, desire, self-loathing, regret, anguish...it was all threatening to overwhelm the vampire. If that happened, then he'd go for Eleanor's throat and fall right into a trap. At least, that's what Gabby suspected.

Either way, her friend was dying, and she wasn't sure what she could do to stop it.

Nye stared down at Isobel and didn't know what to think or feel.

He sat beside her on the bed with his legs outstretched and watched her sleep. If she woke right now and caught him, he was certain she'd have something sharp to say about him being a creepy pervert, and he willed with all his strength for her eyes to open. He'd take the tirade with all the grace he could muster if she just surfaced.

Please, wake up.

She didn't move an inch, her chest rising and falling the only indication she was still with him. Gabby said blame would get him nowhere, but he couldn't help it. He blamed himself for all of it. A mistake he'd made four hundred years ago would cost the life of an innocent woman.

He found her hand and tangled his fingers through hers, his cold skin against her warm, and held on for dear life. Like she was some kind of sleeping beauty, his touch seemed to rouse her. Her eyes fluttered open, and this time, she saw him.

"Nye?" she whispered, his name sounding intoxicating coming from her lips.

"Yes," he replied, squeezing her hand. "I'm here."

"Is this real?" she whispered.

"*It's real.*"

She sighed and moved against the pillow, her eyes screwing shut before she focused on him again.

"Do you remember how you got to the park?" he asked.

She frowned and rolled onto her back, her fingers slipping from his. "She said you loved her."

"Who?"

"Eleanor."

"Eleanor is dead..." he began, knowing it was a lie.

Isobel shook her head. "No... I saw her. I touched her. She's..."

"Isobel, we're talking about something that happened *four hundred years ago*."

"I can't..." she began, sitting up. "I can't do this. You never tell me the truth, and I can't... I don't belong here."

"Isobel," Nye said, moving so he was right beside her. "I will tell you anything you want. I was wrong to shut you out. *I was wrong*."

She scoffed and allowed her body to press against his. "The lord and master of the London vampires apologising to a human woman? Miracles do happen, and it isn't even Christmas."

Her sharp wit practically smacked him around the face, and he smiled. That was the Isobel he knew. The fighter.

"I can ask you anything?"

He nodded. "Anything."

"Was she right? Did you love her?"

"At the time, I was a new vampire," he replied. "Everything felt...*more*."

"Tristan said vampires feel things more than humans do," she murmured, her fingers worrying the edge of the blanket.

Nye felt the sharp sting of jealousy at the thought of Tristan being the one to console her the night he'd lost control.

"I thought I loved her," he went on, his voice sounding stiff. "But now I know it wasn't anywhere close to real love. I was lost for a long time after I turned."

"She gave you meaning," Isobel said, sounding forlorn.

"It was another time," he said. "Another life. I realised many things the day she tried to kill me and a great deal more the day you turned up on my doorstep."

Isobel didn't say a single thing. She opened the drawer beside the bed and pulled out a piece of paper as if she hadn't been listening to a word he'd said.

"No way..." she murmured as she unfolded the paper.

"What's that?" he asked, hoping it wasn't what he thought it was.

She held up the piece of paper, and he recognised the note the Unhallowed had placed on the front door of the mansion to summon the zombie to them. When had she plucked that from the study?

"I can see it now," she said, her voice wavering. "The symbol." She traced the lines with her fingertips, and Nye's heart twisted. "I don't know what it means, but I guess I'm not—"

"Don't say it," Nye said, interrupting her. "It's just the magic... It doesn't mean anything."

"The magic?"

"It's what's making you feel so tired," he explained. "Eleanor... She put a curse on you."

Her expression fell further, and she tossed the paper onto the floor. "*Great*. Just my bloody luck."

"We'll figure it out," Nye said, trying to appease her. "Gabby is working on a spell to remove it, and she's badass. She can do pretty much anything."

Her eyes drooped and she sighed, giving away how tired she actually felt. "I'm sorry."

Nye pulled her hand to his lips. "You've nothing to be sorry for."

"If I'd just listened to you—"

He kissed the palm of her hand, and she stopped mid-sentence. "Gabby's working on it."

"I just wanted... I just wanted..." She turned her face away, but he could see the tears welling in her eyes. "I was so alone... I didn't understand."

"I'm the one who should be apologising," he murmured. "I made you feel this way. I thought I was protecting you...but it was the worst thing I could've done."

Her gaze met his. "Protect me from what? You?" He nodded once, and she sighed. "No…"

"I bit you. That's unforgivable."

"You warned me," she argued.

"It doesn't make it right. I should never have put you in that position…"

Isobel's eyes widened, and her grasp tightened on his hand. "No," she cried. "No, you can't leave me. *Not now*."

Leaning forward, he placed a gentle kiss on her forehead, his heart squeezing when she sighed in contentment. "It's much too late for that," he murmured, his lips brushing against her skin. "Much too late."

CHAPTER 15

When Gabby appeared, Nye didn't know how long he'd lain beside a sleeping Isobel.

Sliding off the bed, he followed her out into the hall, closing the door gently behind him.

"How is she?" the witch murmured as they walked down the hall toward the study—or ground zero as he was beginning to call it.

"Tired," he replied. "I know it's the curse sapping all her energy..."

Gabby nodded, closing them inside the privacy of the study. Nye took one look at the mess she'd created and raised an eyebrow.

Books and papers were strewn everywhere. The shelves that housed a thousand grimoires were pulled apart, dust tickling his nose. Gabby had been hard at work, then.

"Have you found anything?" he asked, turning to

face her. There had to be some spell or remedy inside those pages that could help untangle the curse on Isobel. There were a thousand books with hundreds of spells inside. *There had to be something.*

The witch shook her head, but he could see it in her eyes before she even moved. There was nothing. Nothing... There had to be a witch out there who could help her. If he could just get to Eleanor...

"I called Alex," Gabby declared before he could say anything. "I've told him everything."

"You what?" he exclaimed.

"You've got twelve hours to get your shit together," she said.

The only reason Gabby would have called Isobel's brother was if she... No, there had to be a way. Nothing was permanent. Witches had loopholes and antidotes for *everything.*

"No!" he cried. "You can't let her die. You have to do something! There has to be a witch out there who could—"

"Do you think I want her to die?" she practically shouted at him. "I can't find a way to stop it, Nye. Not in time. Alex deserves to be here. He deserves to know what's happening to his sister."

"Not in time?"

She sighed and lowered her gaze. "It's moving fast. I can feel it from here..."

"This can't be happening," he murmured. "*It can't.*"

He cared deeply for Isobel, there was no use denying it, but love? Love was the ultimate euphoria for a vampire, and it would consume him to the point of addiction if he let it. It would be a constant fight not to bite her again, to taste her sweet blood... Was all that pain worth it? Not his pain...*hers*.

Closing his eyes, he thought about it for a moment. He'd admitted it several times, but he hadn't actually said the words.

Yeah...he was in love with Isobel. Perhaps he should tell her before it was too late.

<hr>

For the second time in as many months, Alex stood at Heathrow Airport on the outskirts of London, hauling his suitcase through the concourse.

And it was the second time he'd dropped everything to come save his sister from vampires getting her involved in their stupid revenge plots. The ironic part? He was a vampire.

He'd sacrificed everything to save Isobel and his friends from the fae hybrid Aed. Allowing Gabby to turn him into a founding vampire, the strongest of their kind, he'd been the only creature able to put the guy down for good. It was either him or Isobel, and there was no hesitation. No way in hell was he allowing his sister to throw away her humanity and everything she'd worked for in Oxford to become...*this*.

Being a vampire, a truly immortal vampire, wasn't a picnic. It was the shittiest thing he'd ever had to deal with. Everywhere he looked, a human snack bar was waiting for him to chow down. He hadn't understood before how his friend Zac had felt with it every day. Zac had always been an inch from losing it, but now Alex understood how painful it was.

The hunger for blood was so strong that sometimes it was hard to resist, but resist he did. Gabby had said it was because he'd been so kind in his human life. He scoffed as the busy airport heaved around him. Some afterlife.

Everything was a million times sharper than he was used to—sight, smell, sound, *feelings*—like the ultimate high-definition television. It didn't take much to piss him off lately, so when he got that call from Gabby less than a day ago, he'd almost flown right off the handle.

Isobel had gotten herself tangled with that upstart Nye, and now she was cursed by a witch who had a grudge against the spy. *Cursed!* When he got to the mansion, he would snap the vampire's neck, and that was being *lenient*.

The taxi ride to Hampstead took the best part of an hour. Peak hour was just hitting as they pulled up out the front of the house, so the drive took less time than usual.

Slamming the door closed, he pulled his suitcase up the path behind him, his vampire senses picking up the tang of magic in the yard. Gabby had said she'd cast about a million wards out here to keep the Unhallowed witches—or were they wraiths?—out.

As he opened the front door and stepped into the foyer, he could sense movement upstairs. Dropping his case, he flew through the house and smashed his way into the study.

His gaze met Nye's, and an unbelievable surge of anger flared inside him. Shooting forward, he fisted his hands into the front of Nye's shirt and shoved him against the wall with enough strength that the plaster cracked.

"What have you done to her?" he snarled. "If she dies, *I will rip you apart.*"

"Alex!" Gabby cried from somewhere far away. "*Calm down.*"

He wasn't listening, his gaze firmly set on the vampire in front of him. "You can understand how important the first few years are for shaping who a vampire is to become, Nye. You're not helping by *seducing my sister.*"

"I care for her," Nye snarled. "I did what I could to protect her. By the time she arrived, it was already too late to send her away."

"*Bullshit.*"

"I'm trying to lead this city," Nye said, shoving him hard enough that his grip loosened. "I have eyes on me all the time, and none of them are good, Alex. They all want the power I now have, and they'd do anything to get it. I kept her here so I could save her from this."

"And you got her cursed anyway!" Alex roared.

Nye stepped up into Alex's face and stared him down. "I won't rest until I find a way to save her."

"You love her. So that's what this is about, huh? Your crazy ex has resurrected herself and is going after my sister to get back at you. If you'd just kept it in your pants back in Oxford, then she wouldn't have come here at all!"

"She came here to see you!" Nye roared. "If you hadn't left without telling her, then she wouldn't have come."

"*Stop it!*" Gabby shrieked, shoving between them. Squeezing between the two men, she tried to push them apart, but they were like marble statues. They didn't budge an inch.

"It doesn't matter how she got here," she went on. "*It doesn't matter*. We need to find a way to buy us some time."

"But you said..." Nye began, glancing at her.

"I know, but if there's a way to slow the spread, then it might give us the time to find a cure."

"Have you tried vampire blood?" Alex asked.

"It won't work," Nye declared, glaring at him. "Our blood only heals physical wounds, not magical ones."

"Besides," Gabby added. "If she dies with vampire blood in her system, she'll turn..."

"I don't know about you, but I'd like to preserve her

humanity at all costs," Nye snapped. "Neither of us had a choice. Vampirism isn't a cure all."

"I wouldn't wish this on my worst enemy," Alex fired back just as quickly.

"Fighting about it isn't solving anything," Gabby interjected. Turning to Alex, she said, "You should go see her."

Nodding, Alex backed away from the man who'd gotten his sister into this mess. This wasn't over between them, not by a long shot. Nye was a smart guy, so he'd understand that this was only the beginning. They had an eternity to hate one another, after all.

Glancing at him, Alex delivered a warning, and if he were smart enough, the spy would heed it. "If you care for her like you claim, you'll leave her alone. *For good.*"

Nye's expression didn't change, but Alex knew he'd hit him where it hurt the most. He could see it in everything the spy did...he was in love with his sister, and Alex didn't know what the hell he thought about that. Isobel didn't belong in this world.

Opening the door to his sister's room, he stepped inside.

Instantly, he sensed her lying on the bed, her breathing shallow as she slept soundly. Not even the fight down the hall had roused her.

Sitting beside her, Alex pulled her hand into his and sighed. He could dwell on whose fault it was as much as he wanted, but it didn't change the fact that what's done is done. Right now, they had to find a way to remove the curse before it was too late.

Her eyes fluttered open, and she stared at him for what felt like an age before she spoke. "Alex?"

"The one and only."

"What are you doing here?"

"Don't sound so surprised," he replied with a smile. "You're my big sister."

Isobel pushed herself up so that she sat next to him, her fingers tightening around his. "Gabby must've told you because no way in hell Nye would've squealed."

"Yeah, what's up with that?" he asked, raising his eyebrows. "*Seriously?*"

"Shut up," she drawled. "Like you have immaculate taste in women."

"But a vampire, Izzy? What happened to having a family?"

"Who said I wanted to squeeze a baby out of my vagina?" She rolled her eyes.

"*Gross.*"

They sat in silence for a while, neither of them knowing what to say considering the weight that was currently hanging over their heads.

"They can't find a way to stop it, can they?" Isobel asked, closing her eyes. "That's why you came back."

"Don't say that," he said, pulling her in for a hug. "Just don't."

"I won't say it if you don't give me false hope," she retorted, her voice wavering.

Alex stroked her hair, listening to her heart beating inside her chest and her tight breaths. She was trying not to cry.

"Whatever happens, I'm going to make them pay," he whispered. "Every single one of them."

CHAPTER 16

Nye stared down at the bloody remains of Sabine and wrinkled his nose.

Whoever killed the poor girl hadn't been elegant about it. Her throat had been torn open and her body drained by a sloppy eater—blood was splattered and smeared everywhere, the little flat she'd lived and worked in covered with the stuff.

The whole place was set up as one massive altar with candles, runes, crystals, and herbs littered everywhere. A large bookcase sat against one wall, overflowing with jars full of potions, dried herbs, and all kinds of ingredients the witch had used to make the bullshit potions she'd sold to unscrupulous humans desperate for some kind of cure all to their mundane problems. Considering the roll of fifty-pound notes he'd found stashed in a corner, she was raking it in with her fakery. Ironic considering she was the real deal, and he'd paid her well over the years. Whatever did she spend her money on?

"It could've been another one of those zombies," Alex said, his gaze running over the shelves of tinctures.

"Perhaps," Nye replied. "There isn't any solid proof, and the neighbour didn't hear a thing. The one that attacked the mansion had no wits about it."

"Then someone might've compelled her to forget."

Nye snorted and turned away from Sabine's corpse. If that was the case, then the Unhallowed had a living, breathing, sane vampire working for them, which didn't bode well. With every minute that passed, this predicament was getting more out of control.

"So what now, Your Majesty?" the founder asked with an air of sarcasm.

Nye rolled his eyes and picked up Sabine's grimoire. Flipping through the pages, he wondered if she had anyone left to give it to. She wasn't aligned to any coven he knew of. Another tome for Gabby's shelves perhaps.

"Have you been practicing your compulsion?" he asked Alex as he snapped the book shut.

The vampire shrugged. "A little."

With no leads on who killed Sabine, there was nothing else for them do but wait for Gabby, so the two vampires could pay a few insubordinate vampires a visit. Since Alex was a founder, he could compel vampires...a very handy skill to have at one's disposal. With the London vampires united, they could focus all their energy on Isobel and the Unhallowed.

"Then it may be in our best interests to squash a few annoying vampires," Nye said, glancing at him. "While the going is good."

Alex scowled. "Why should I help you cement your power? What's stopping me from telling them to rip you to pieces?"

"Your sister," Nye replied.

"*Who you will leave alone.*"

"Even if I sever ties, they won't stop. It's much too late to cut and run, Alex. Besides, she's tied more closely to you than she is to me." Nye slipped the grimoire under his arm. "Isobel is known now. If she's not used to get to me, she'll be used to get to you. The more secure my rule of the London vampires is, the better I can protect her."

"Compulsion to get people to follow you?" Alex rolled his eyes.

"I don't have time to do it the right way," he shot back. "We both want the same thing, Alex."

"I don't understand how she could have any feelings toward you," Alex muttered, pushing past him.

Too tired to think of a comeback, Nye narrowed his eyes and followed him outside to the car. Neither could he.

When they returned to the mansion, Gabby was still buried in her grimoires, dwarfed behind the mahogany desk.

Nye knelt before her and pried the book from her tired fingers, setting it on the smallest pile.

"Have you slept?" Alex asked, leaning against the desk.

The witch shook her head. "Not really. I don't have time to sleep."

"Have you made any progress since we left?" Nye prompted, rising to his feet.

"This," Gabby said, plucking a piece of paper from between the pages of a grimoire.

"That's the symbol the Unhallowed put on the door to lure their creature," Nye said warily as she placed it on the desk. "What's that got to do with anything?"

"A great deal," she replied. "It's more than a tether. It's a map."

Alex leaned over the desk and peered at the markings. "How do you figure that? It looks like a bunch of scribbles if you ask me."

"Here," Gabby began, tracing her finger over the lines. "I didn't see it at first, but it's like one of those Magic Eye puzzles."

"Great," Nye scoffed. "Another witchy puzzle."

"These signify ley lines," she went on, ignoring his quip. "The mark at the bottom is for resurrection, which you were right about, but it also gives us a clue as to where the Unhallowed might be...or at least, where they got the power to cast the spell."

"Got the power? They're already witches," Alex said, his brow furrowing.

"They were once," Nye said. "But now they're something nastier."

"Wraiths," Gabby said simply. "They need a power source to do any significant spell work, and ley lines are an easy mark."

Alex still didn't quite understand. "What's a ley line?"

"Ley lines circle the earth, connecting sacred sites that have an abundance of earth and spirit energy," Gabby explained. "Places like churches, burial sites, and standing stones were all built over them in ancient times, long before witches were created. They were places of importance to the Celestines because of their direct conduit to their souls and that of the earth and universe. They travel across the earth in straight lines."

"And the Unhallowed have found a way to leech off that power?" Alex asked.

She nodded. "There are many across the countryside, but this spell holds the key to which one they used."

"And where is it?" Nye asked, his mind mulling over this new information.

"About twenty minutes outside of London to the east," the witch replied, showing him the location on her phone. "A stone circle is there, dating back a few thousand years. The perfect place to launch their assault from if you ask me."

"We should check it out," Alex said.

"I don't think that's wise," Nye declared. "Eleanor took down Tristan without even blinking."

"But I'm a founder."

"Still wouldn't risk it."

"He's right," Gabby agreed. "I'm not even sure how to fight a bunch of wraiths. We can't risk it without knowing more."

"What about the curse?" Alex asked, turning to the witch. "Have you worked out how to slow it?"

"I don't think I can," Gabby replied, rubbing her eyes. "At least, not enough to buy us the time I need to find a cure...if there is one."

"So we just sit here and watch Isobel slip away?" Alex exclaimed. "There must be something we can do."

Nye glanced at the door and back again. There was something he could do to save her. The only thing any of them could do to get the Unhallowed to lift the curse in time. Nye had to admit defeat and turn himself over.

It would destroy Isobel, but she would be alive and safe. Alex and Gabby would protect her, and the Unhallowed would disappear once they had his head on a pike. Why fight the inevitable?

Thanks to Gabby, he knew exactly where to go to find Eleanor. All that was left to do was leave.

"Fuck this," he cursed, rising to his feet.

"Don't you even think of doing something stupid," Gabby snapped at him.

"No, Gabby. I'm going to check on Isobel and then twiddle my thumbs while you bang your head against the wall," he retorted and strode from the room before anyone could even think of stopping him from seeing Isobel.

His gaze met Tristan's as he stepped out into the hall. *There was a sight for sore eyes.*

"Where the hell have you been?" he asked.

The knight shrugged, totally out of profound metaphors for the first time in his life.

"You need a tighter leash, *dog*," Nye snarled and shoved past him.

Behind him, he heard the study door open as Tristan disappeared inside and then voices as they filled him in on the events he'd missed.

Nye didn't care what they did anymore. He supposed Tristan would step up as leader of the London vampires. There was no one else in their circle capable of handling the position. Either way, it was out of his control.

Easing Isobel's bedroom door open, he ghosted across to her bedside. She stirred as if she sensed his presence, and her eyes opened.

"Hey," she murmured, her lips curving into a smile.

"Hey," he replied, sitting beside her and smoothing her rumpled hair away from her face. "How are you feeling?"

"*Shit.*"

Leaning down, he placed a soft kiss against her forehead. It was no use hiding his affection now. Not if this was going to be the last time he saw her sweet face.

"I just wanted to see you before I stepped out," he said.

"Where are you going?"

"Just an errand. Nothing special," he replied, his heart sinking.

Her eyes drooped. "Oh..."

"Sleep," he said, tugging up her blankets. "You'll feel better soon."

She murmured something incomprehensible as she slipped into her dreams once more. Her condition was worsening, and her waking moments were becoming less frequent...there was no time to lose.

"Goodbye, Isobel," he murmured with all the conviction he could muster. She'd be well soon enough. He'd make sure of it.

Setting his phone on the bedside table, he left her to rest, knowing that when she woke, she would be free of the curse.

Closing the bedroom door behind him, he went downstairs and outside into the night, sliding into one of the many cars Regulus had left to Gabby.

Nobody followed or tried to stop him, but why

would they? Gabby knew it. Alex knew it. Even Tristan knew it. This was the only way to save them all. Wasn't love about sacrifice?

Gunning the engine, he pulled out of the garage and onto the road, powering toward his destiny.

CHAPTER 17

Nye breathed deeply as he crossed the field, the air sweet with the lingering summer sun.

Overhead, the moon was only just visible, its last quarter hanging low in the sky and casting little light over his final march. Ahead, the six fingers of the standing stones the map had led him to broke up the straight horizon.

It was here that he hoped to find Eleanor so he could put this feud to rest. He was counting on it.

As Nye approached, he was keenly aware that the temperature was dropping. With every step, the air became ice, and it reminded him of the cold nothingness that awaited him in death. *True* death.

Lingering at the edge of the stones, he waited in the darkness. He was alone in the physical sense, yet all around him, he felt the presence of a lingering anger and the charge in the air that always preceded a witch's appearance. They were here.

As he waited for them to show their faces, he cast his gaze over the site of his final stand. There was no way out, but he still looked for one.

The standing stones were a circle of six jagged bluestone slabs with a smaller stone in the centre, which he understood was called the Blood Stone in this kind of formation. During the Middle Ages, they had been repurposed by some fanatical groups as places of sacrifice...*human* sacrifice. On a few occasions, he'd put a stop to the barbaric practice while in service to the English Crown. Now they'd been recycled yet again—this time, as a supernatural battery for that bitch Eleanor and her coven of wraiths.

A plot four hundred years in the making... Eleanor had conviction—he'd give her that.

"Nye Saer," a voice purred from behind him.

He stilled at the sound of Eleanor's voice but didn't turn. She stepped around him and glided into the stone circle, lifting her right hand. Clicking her fingers, flame erupted, engulfing the torches that had been placed in the ground between each bluestone slab.

He narrowed his eyes at the sight of her in modern clothing, her hair wild and her eyes darkened with makeup. Someone as vain as Eleanor must revel in the trappings of modern fashion. Women were freer than they'd ever been throughout history, even if they were harbouring a supernatural secret.

"Come," she said, curling her finger to gesture him forward. "I'm glad you're here."

Stepping into the light, he glared at the witch with all the disdain he could muster. "You know why I'm here. I want proof that you've lifted the curse before I let you have me, or I'll take your head...and this time, I won't be so *efficient* about it."

"What a queer thing it is for a vampire to love a human," she said, regarding him. "You would give up your eternity so Isobel might live, what...a handful of years?"

"If you understood what love is, Eleanor, you'd understand why."

He saw the anger in her gaze, and he felt nothing. He wanted to fight, but he knew it was useless. He stood in her domain, the place where she was most powerful. Even with Gabby at his side, he couldn't win. To go up against Eleanor now was foolish.

"I've been watching you for a very long time, Nye," she began, her eyes shining with malice. "The murders. The hunting. How you carried out a Roman's orders without question. The same Roman who helped you *cut off my head.*"

"Looks like you got it back," he retorted, not missing a beat.

Eleanor snorted. "How could a man like you love a woman like that?"

He laughed at the irony. "What? Are you jealous?"

Her lip curled in anger, and she turned away.

"Remove the curse on Isobel, and I am yours to do with what you will."

Eleanor seemed to ignore his demands and placed her palm against the standing stone before her. Her head lowered, and she began to chant in the language of the witches. The language given to them as gifts from the Celestines...from his friend Aya. It was sickening to hear, knowing what Eleanor had become. Everything that had made the Unhallowed witches had been forsaken so they could live forever in pursuit of a single goal. Revenge.

"It is done," she said, turning to face him once more.

"I want proof," he demanded. "Your words mean nothing to me."

"Kneel," she commanded. When he didn't move to spite her, she held up her hand and roared, "*Kneel!*"

Pain tore through his head, and his knees buckled beneath him as her power ripped into his body.

"You want proof?" she asked, standing before him. "*Here is your proof.*"

Her palm slammed against his forehead, and an image burst into his mind's eye. Eleanor wasn't gentle about it as the vision was forced into the deepest parts of his brain, making it feel like his head was being split in two...but he saw her. *Isobel.*

She lay in her bed at the mansion, sleeping just as he'd left her earlier. Gabby was beside her, asleep in the armchair someone had moved from the opposite end of the room. Isobel stirred, and then her eyes fluttered open. As if she'd been drowning and starved for oxygen, she pulled in a sharp breath and sat up, a single word on her lips... *Nye.*

Eleanor tore the vision away just as brutally as she'd given it, and he fell forward, his palms connecting with the ground.

"You have your proof," the wraith snarled. "Now let's get on with it, shall we? We have a long night ahead of us, Nye Saer."

She turned and began walking away as five figures appeared in the darkness before her. Glancing up, he tried to focus on their forms, but it was like they weren't even there. They looked human, but they were made up of shadow...neither here nor there. Every so often, a burst of light appeared inside their bodies, like a lightning storm was brewing. He'd never seen anything like them in his entire life, and he'd seen some pretty crazy things. This must be the Unhallowed in their true form. There was no other explanation.

It was five shades of fucked up if you asked him.

Nye was powerless as the wraiths approached, his body frozen as he was lifted by an unknown force and laid out on the Blood Stone. So this was how she was going to exact her revenge. By carving him up into little pieces.

No one was coming to help him, but it was how he wanted it. No one else had to get hurt.

He would endure alone knowing he'd saved Isobel from the darkness.

That would get him through.

Gabby's dreams took her far that night.

After Nye left the study, Tristan had appeared, and together, they'd attempted to work out a plan to take out the Unhallowed at the source. Nothing any of them proposed was happening any time soon. Attacking the wraiths at the source of their power was the ultimate definition of stupid. They had to figure out a way to lure them into the open, and then they could sever them from the ley line...*maybe*.

It was all trial and error, but they didn't have time for the error part. Not when Isobel was fading.

Gabby's dreams carried her to her memories of the spirit world. She'd walked through the between place where all supernatural souls resided, the veil between the here and the hereafter, in search of Katrin the Betrayer. She'd been able to talk to the founding witch only because of their shared affinity in all things Roman. She'd had her love for Regulus and Katrin's grimoire, which was the only thing that had led her to the witch.

Going into the spirit realm now would be risky. The Unhallowed's magic worked on a spiritual level, and there was no way of telling where the wraiths could walk.

A sharp gasp of air roused her from her dreams, and Gabby sat up in the chair, rubbing her tired eyes.

Isobel was sitting up in bed, a wild look in her eyes. *What the hell was happening?*

"*Nye*," Isobel whispered, her fingers tightening around the blankets that had covered her.

She reached out for Izzy, and when her fingers connected with her skin, she was zapped with a bolt of static electricity that had her snatching her hand back. That's when Gabby realised what Nye had done.

"Tristan!" she shrieked, bolting from the room.

The knight materialised in the hall and grasped her shoulders. "What's happened?"

"Isobel's awake..." she began. "Like *awake*."

"What?" He let her go and ran a hand over his face. "I don't like the look on your face, Gabby."

"Nye... Where is he?" Tristan's expression fell, and Gabby shoved past him, heading for the study. "Shit!"

Alex appeared behind them, roused by the commotion. "What's going on?"

"The curse is gone. I can't feel it in her anymore," Gabby replied.

The founder's eyes widened as he followed her into the study. "Isobel's awake?"

"Yes," she muttered, fumbling through the papers on the desk, oblivious to the two vampires behind her.

"Gabby?"

They glanced up at Isobel, who'd staggered down the hall and was now leaning against the doorway of the study, looking like she'd been through hell and back. In a way, she had.

Tristan shot forward and threaded his arm around her back. Helping her into the room, he set her gently into one of the armchairs by the fireplace.

"What's going on?" she asked again as Alex draped a blanket across her lap. "I don't feel tired anymore..."

Gabby glanced uncertainly at Tristan while Alex doted on his sister, smoothing her tangled hair.

"Tell me!" Izzy practically shouted at them.

"It wasn't me," she said after a moment of awkward silence. "I didn't lift the curse."

Isobel's hand flew to her mouth. "Then he... He..."

"He sacrificed himself for you," Alex said, looking totally shocked. "He did... He was telling me the truth..."

"No!" she exclaimed, her bother's words not even registering. "We have to get him back!"

"Isobel—"

"Shut up, Alex," she snapped, flinging the blanket aside and practically launching herself from the chair. "I didn't ask him to do this! I didn't want him to! *I need him back!*"

Alex threw his arms round her, trying to soothe her rising desperation, but she pushed against him.

"Without Nye, who is going to lead this shithole of a city?" she cried. "No one! I didn't even... I didn't even get to... We need him!" She shook her head, wiping away her frustrated tears even as Alex held her in his arms. "He's made the ultimate sacrifice...for me. A puny weakling of a human being. It can't be too late to save him. *We have to try.*"

"You can say it, Izzy," Alex murmured.

"Say what?"

"What you're feeling."

"I just did!" She glanced at Gabby and Tristan, and her shoulders sank. "I need him back…"

Gabby plucked the parchment off the desktop, the one that contained the map to the standing stones, and cast her gaze over the runes. Isobel's fiery conviction and her own passionate entanglement with Regulus had all but convinced her.

"They've taken him to the Keeping Place," she said, holding up the parchment. "It's there they'll exact their revenge…"

"What the hell is the Keeping Place?" Alex asked, letting Isobel go.

"The standing stones, I guess." Gabby shrugged.

"Then what are we waiting for?" Isobel asked. "*Let's go!*"

"Oh no," her brother declared. "You're not going anywhere."

Izzy faced him off. "Try to stop me."

Gabby could see fighting her was useless. It was going to be dangerous, but Isobel being there might just be the thing that turned the tide for Nye. She had a good idea how much suffering the Unhallowed would subject him to and how long they'd draw it out, so he'd need something stronger than life itself to pull him back. He would fight for Isobel, knowing that she was fighting just as hard.

"She's coming," Gabby said, using the force of her power behind her command.

The two vampires stilled, sensing the energy in the air, and it was decided. For better or worse.

Isobel nodded, squaring her jaw. "Let's go get that bitch and tear her a new one."

CHAPTER 18

One thing Gabby had learned since becoming a witch was you never went into a magical fight without some preparation.

Witches were fond of loopholes, counter-spells, and the will of nature, so there had to be some ace she could pull out of her sleeve. There was no doubt in her mind they would have to face Eleanor and her coven of Unhallowed wraiths before the night was through. It was entirely possible they were too late to save Nye. Glancing at Isobel, who sat next to her in the back of the car, she had to believe it wasn't an option.

Tristan was driving, and Alex was in the passenger seat, the glow of his cell phone bright in the darkness. Outside, the city had melted into sprawling countryside as they ventured off the main highway and through narrow country lanes on their way to the stone circle.

Gabby focused her energy on her grimoire where

she'd documented everything she'd been through as a witch. From her humble beginnings lighting candles all the way to the fae hybrid she'd hunted with Regulus. Finally, the newest pages contained her notes and speculations on the Unhallowed...and she had a lot of those. Wild fairy tales with no basis in reality.

One thing that disturbed her was the location of the stone circle. It didn't just sit on a ley line but was a place where three of those lines intersected. Three points of power all culminating underneath the Stone Age monument, giving the Unhallowed the equivalent of an all-you-can-eat buffet, which explained a great deal about the kind of magic they were able to pull off considering they weren't supposed to have human forms.

That was another thing that gave Gabby the creeps. No one had seen a wraith for a thousand years, but in all the grimoires that had spoken about their kind, they described them as 'clouds of thunder and lightning, retaining the shape of what they once were,' which was men and women. For Eleanor to appear in her human form there had to be some serious power behind the coven. The ley lines explained it.

For all the theories she held, none of them helped her with how to kill one of these things. When they got to the stone circle, what was she going to do?

"How much further?" Isobel asked, leaning forward.

"Not far," Alex replied. "Ten minutes."

Gabby glanced at her friend. "Stay with Alex when we get there. I don't know what we'll find."

"What's the plan?" Tristan asked, glancing at her in the rearview mirror.

"I don't know how to kill them," she replied. "Not for sure. I can try to slow them down and buy us time..."

"So we do a smash and grab," Alex said. "Gabby distracts them with her awesomeness, and we grab Nye. Then we get back to the mansion where it's safe and sound. We can kick their asses another day when we have a surefire way of sending those bitches to hell."

"I like the sound of that," Tristan said in agreement.

Gabby turned to Isobel, who was staring out the window at the passing countryside. The whole time they'd been in the car, she hadn't uttered a word, lost in her own thoughts and fears. If it were Regulus in the clutches of the Unhallowed, she'd be just as passionate about saving him. They'd had a love that crossed the walls hatred had placed between their kinds... Witches and vampires. It was the same with humans. The predator and the prey. The sun and the moon. Good and evil.

If Gabby could learn only one thing from this crazy quest, it was that love conquered all, even when the union was the deadliest of them all. Nye and Isobel would have the time she didn't have with Regulus. It seemed fitting in the wake of her loss, but with everything in this crazy world of witches and vampires, it would come with a price. She was certain of it.

"Isobel?" she asked, nudging her friend.

"Huh?" Isobel glanced at Gabby, a faraway look in her eyes.

"He might be in a bad way," she said gently. "And you might be the only one of us who can get through to him. Are you up for it?"

Isobel nodded furiously, her shoulders squaring. "I'll do whatever it takes."

"Stick with Alex," she said. "He'll have your back and get you to Nye. Leave the Unhallowed to me."

"Who's got your back?" Izzy asked.

Gabby smiled, allowing her power to thrum in her veins. "I've got my own. Don't worry about me."

As Tristan turned the car off the sealed road and onto a dirt track, Gabby contemplated the scene that was about to unfold. They were walking into a war zone. The Unhallowed had all the advantage, and they had none...but maybe, *just maybe*, they had underestimated how powerful she was. Even she didn't know how deep her gifts ran. Even when she went up against Aed, the most powerful hybrid that had ever existed, she hadn't reached all the way inside her soul.

But the deeper she went, the riskier it became. With great power came darkness, no matter how good one claimed to be. She'd used her dark power once before, back when Arturius had held her against her will and used his witches to try to corrupt her, and it had taken a bolt of Aya's Celestine power to bring her back. With time, the power had returned—the energy the hybrid used only wilting the leaves, not killing the root...and the plant had begun to grow anew.

If Gabby lost herself to it now, she knew there was no coming back. Was she willing to risk it so Nye and Isobel had a chance to love one another? It was pointless even contemplating it because she already knew the answer.

She closed her grimoire and slid it underneath the seat in front of her for safekeeping, preparing herself for the storm to come.

Perhaps it was past time to find out how deep her power really ran.

***

Nye stared up at the night sky, the orange light from the torches surrounding the stone circle glowing in his peripheral vision. He lay on the Blood Stone, fixed in place by magic and bound to his fate.

He sensed movement all around as the Unhallowed worked their ritual. They muttered under their breaths—probably some indecipherable witch talk that spoke to the dark places Gabby had told him about. Forbidden spirit magic that was an insult to everything she was.

Whatever the Unhallowed had in store for his soul, it wasn't anything good, and they weren't letting him in on the punch line. Eternal damnation sounded horrific, but who was alive to tell anyone what it was really like? Was there such a thing, or was the whole notion just dreamed up by men and women who were afraid of the unknown? Fear was a powerful motivator, one he'd used only the day before. Vampires dealt in the stuff like humans thirsted for money.

He tensed as Eleanor climbed atop his body, straddling his waist like a lover. Her cold fingers curled around the hem of his shirt and ripped, buttons popping as she exposed his chest.

"Kinky," he muttered, not wanting to make this easy for her. "You've been dreaming about getting in my pants again for four hundred years, haven't you? Are you sure you want your wraith-ey friends to watch? Or are you into exhibitionism now?"

Eleanor laughed, splaying her hands on his stomach. He thought his skin was cold but hers felt like the chill of death itself and a universe apart from the ice he carried in his veins.

"Since you're sitting right on my sweet spot," he went on, "you're probably thinking I've got performance issues, but too bad for you because I'm not into soul-sucking wraiths."

"It's too late, Nye," she replied, stroking her fingers across the rise and dip of his abs. "Your words are meaningless."

"I feel sorry for you," he drawled, taking one last stab. "You'll never find love, Eleanor. You're not capable of feeling it for anything but yourself and the evil you've created. If you think that's true love, then you're sorely mistaken."

Her expression tightened. "You think because I lifted the curse on your precious human she's safe forever? Are you really that naive?"

"If you even try to harm her again, you won't get far," he snarled. "Gabby and Tristan—"

"Tristan?" Eleanor asked with a laugh. "He was the easiest of all to manipulate. *How do you think Isobel got out of the house?*"

Nye's eyes widened.

"That's right, love," she purred. "I compelled him to kill your witch, and right now...he's with your precious Isobel. Imagine what I could make him do to her."

Sabine... Tristan had killed Sabine! The night he was attacked by Eleanor, she hadn't tried to siphon him at all...she'd put a compulsion on him to get inside the mansion and hit them all where it hurt. It explained why the knight had been missing for two days. *Shit!*

"You'll never get away with it," he said. "*They won't allow it.*"

Leaning over him, Eleanor curled her arms around his neck like a lover, her lips pressing against his ear. He tried to push against her, to dislodge her poisonous hands, but he was paralysed. *Bitch!*

She nipped at his ear before whispering, "How does it feel to know your sacrifice was for nothing?"

Nye thrashed—or at least, he did on the inside—and spat at her, "*I hope you burn in hell.*"

"Come, sisters," she declared, returning to a seated position on his lap.

The wraiths moved out of the shadows and approached the Blood Stone. They leaned over him, all six witches looking down on him with disdain from the human faces they'd taken on, the cloud of thunder and lightning that were their true forms having all but disappeared.

"The circle is complete," Eleanor said to the others. "Now it is time to begin."

Nye never believed it when people told stories of their lives flashing before their eyes when certain death was upon them. He had a great deal of life to fast-forward through and not enough time to relive it all considering his predicament, but try as he might to forget, some memories surfaced.

Oddly enough, the first thing he saw was the little girl he'd tried to help in the bottom reaches of the Tower of London. The little girl who'd killed a whole slew of humans in her desperate need for blood, and the same who saw his kindness as something to be preserved. He'd been compelled and turned into a beast by a *child*. A child who didn't understand what she had become, so she had given in to the monster.

He'd been lost at the time, forced into a semblance of retirement because of the scar that split his face. His life had been about blending into shadows, obtaining information and striking, being one of many, silent and deadly... He was marked and no longer fit for duty because of it. Those feelings had crossed with him into his next life...until he met Eleanor. The rest was a history that could not be unwritten.

What a miserable story with a miserable end.

But of all the memories in his mind, he finished with Isobel and her unfaltering fearlessness in Oxford all those months ago. The kiss they shared at the mansion haunted him still, even with its unfortunate end. Everything about her was reminiscent of flame... He imagined her in all her glory and held her image close. She was in even more danger, and he was the only one who knew it.

Isobel.

Eleanor smiled, her lips curling in triumph as she raised a dagger high into the star-studded sky.

When the point of the blade pierced his flesh and began dragging, cutting him open in an elaborate design, he never gave her the satisfaction of hearing him suffer.

He never would.

CHAPTER 19

"We're here."

Gabby glanced up at the sound of Alex's voice. Tristan had brought the car to a halt behind another car parked on the dark track. *Nye.*

"Let's do this," Gabby said. "We approach together."

"I suggest using stealth," Tristan advised, opening his door. "We are goin' in at a disadvantage."

"Agreed," Gabby chimed in.

They assembled outside the car, and Alex took his sister's hand. "Stick with me, Izzy. I just got you back from the Unhallowed's curse, and I'm not going to let them take you again."

"Neither am I," she replied. "Not if I can help it."

Turning her attention onto the field beside the track, Gabby saw the glow at the top of the rise. That had to be it. It was the only smudge against the night, the only other light coming from the moon that hung low in the sky, its last quarter holding on with silver fingers.

Flame illuminated the stone circle as they crossed the field, the long fingers of bluestone stretching into the sky. Even at the distance they were, Gabby could feel the rush of energy in the air. Whatever the Unhallowed were doing to Nye, they were still in the midst of their revenge. *It wasn't too late.*

She raised her hand, alerting the others as the emanations grew. "Six," she whispered just loud enough for the two vampires to hear. She sensed the presence of each wraith, all of them focused on a single point in the centre of their circle.

Ancient monuments like these usually had a central point, a flat stone used as an altar, and that was where Nye had to be. The central point directly over the ley lines would anchor the Unhallowed's power, and whatever they were doing to him would be more potent there.

Finally, they reached the outer circle of stones. Gabby saw the six witches—or wraiths, somehow in human form—but she was drawn to the body that lay on the Blood Stone within their circle.

Nye.

Blood coated his chest, and from this distance, she couldn't see what they'd carved there, but it was nasty. His gaze was fixed on the sky, his body paralysed. She felt Isobel stiffen beside her at the sight of the vampire, and Alex tugged her back.

If they didn't do anything, Nye was done for. They'd drain his energy until he was nothing but a husk. What was stopping them from resurrecting his corpse to come back and take Isobel? Nothing. They'd lured Nye here, but who said they'd keep their word once they'd gotten what they wanted? Gabby didn't trust those witches as far as she could throw them.

It was way past time to kick some Unhallowed ass.

Gabby strode forward into the stone circle and raised her hand, muttering a spell under her breath. The Unhallowed were caught unawares, too wrapped up in their ritual to feel her presence, and they fell to the ground like stones as her power collided with them.

It was the chance Alex and Tristan needed to run forward, grab Nye, and drag him from the stone. The spell holding him in place was broken, allowing them to pull him to safety. He moaned loudly, beginning to writhe against the grasp of his friends as whatever ritual had been weaved over him was severed.

The wraiths clambered to their feet as Gabby stood her ground, Eleanor at the front of the pack, her eyes wild with anger.

"*You*," she snarled, her eyes glowing with a white fire Gabby had never seen before. "You'll pay for this Gabrielle Cohen. I don't care who you are to *them*, you will join Nye in hell."

Them? Somehow, Gabby didn't think she meant the three vampires and one human who were now behind her, but there was no time to contemplate or ask empty questions. Eleanor was pissed, and the collective group of wraiths were forming a link to fire back…and it was going to be an epic battle of wills.

They'd snatched Nye, but they still had the getting away part to pull off.

"You may have tricked Nye into giving himself up to you, but I won't let you have him without a fight," Gabby declared, facing off with the six wraiths. "You know who I am, but the world hasn't seen what I can do yet."

"Am I meant to fear you?" Eleanor asked, raising her hands. "Because your words are empty. Have you tapped into a ley line before, Gabrielle? It's so *invigorating*."

Eleanor's hand shot out, and Gabby reacted instantly. Reaching inside herself, she grasped the thread that bound the darkness inside her and pulled. *Hard.*

As the ground began to shudder beneath her feet, the wraiths glanced at one another, and Eleanor's hand dropped before she could strike. The earth splintered and rose into the air, creating a perfect circle around the ancient site. It hovered there for a moment before slowly beginning to turn.

"What…" Eleanor said, glancing around wildly.

"The earth is fighting back," Gabby said, flicking her wrist. "It doesn't like it when an evil bitch like you steals its power."

The debris began to rotate faster and faster until a whirlwind surrounded the entire stone circle.

"Gabby, you better know what you're doing," she heard Alex shout from behind her.

Truthfully, she wasn't sure where this was going at all. The dark power inside of her had risen up and taken control, and she was going with the flow.

The Unhallowed stood before her and joined hands, linking their power together and pooling it within Eleanor.

"Let's see how strong you really are, Gabrielle," she declared, letting her arrogance shine. "One witch against six wraiths. I wonder who's going to win."

Gabby pushed down the urge to roll her eyes and focused her will on the wraiths. *Disappear, begone, and go back to the hole you crawled out from!*

They fought a silent battle as the earth tried to pull itself away from the ley line, but something was stopping it from breaking free. The tornado heaved around them, angry and wild, powering the dark coil of energy inside her. Willing it toward her targets, they forced her back and she them in turn.

She fought with everything she had, but together, she feared they were too much for her. Even calling on the darkness hadn't done much to slow the Unhallowed's advance.

It was a battle of wills within the confines of the stone circle, the tornado whipping around and around, kicking up debris and sending it flying.

Gabby was aware her friends were behind her, trapped within the boundary and unable to escape.

From someplace faraway, she was aware Nye had begun to move, dragging himself across the circle toward the Unhallowed.

"*What are you doin'?*" Tristan exclaimed, trying to pull him back, but he was met with a kick to the face.

"Get off me!" Nye cried.

"Nye!" Isobel pleaded, but he didn't listen, not even to her.

Gabby couldn't move to stop him since she was locked in the battle against the wraiths. If she slipped for even one moment, they were done.

Nye collapsed beside the Blood Stone and fumbled in the dirt, raising the ire of the Unhallowed and Eleanor, but there was nothing they could do. Gabby had them trapped for the time being, or at least until one of them faltered. What was Nye up to?

He clutched a dagger in his hands, blood dripping from the open wound in his chest. Eleanor pushed against Gabby's power with everything she had, but the darkness the witch had conjured held her in check.

As Nye raised the dagger, Isobel called out.

"What are you doing?" she yelled, her voice carrying off into the wind.

"I'll come back," he replied, his eyes glassy. "*This isn't the end...*"

"Isobel, stay back!" Alex exclaimed, wrapping his arms around his sister.

"No!" she screeched. "Let me go!"

Gabby didn't have the energy to weigh in on another fight. The Unhallowed hadn't slowed, but she could feel their power waning.

Nye raised the dagger and thrust the blade into his chest. The steel slammed into his heart, and Isobel screamed, thrashing against Alex's grip.

Nye's eyes glazed over, and he gasped as the life left his body, his fingers slipping from the hilt...then he fell to the ground.

The exact moment his heart stopped beating, Gabby felt the Unhallowed falter. Finally, she understood why they had lured Nye here. Their revenge wasn't a swift or painful death. They were using his immortality and ability to heal for a darker purpose. He was a thing to them... A slave, sacrifice... and would be for eternity. That was the Unhallowed's revenge.

Nye was the tether, and by ending his life, he'd severed their connection to the deeper power of the earth. The harder they fought against Gabby without it, the faster their reserve power would deplete. They would have to run or face an eternity of nothing if they failed in subduing her.

No prizes for guessing which option they took.

The force surrounding Gabby dissolved, the wind pulling it away until it was no more. The Unhallowed began shedding their human forms, even Eleanor, and one by one, they flung themselves into the twister that surrounded the stone circle. She felt them disappear, their energy popping and fizzing into nothing as they fled.

Utterly spent, Gabby dropped her arms and fell to her knees in the dirt, tears streaming from her eyes. It wasn't the end of them, but for now, their power source was fried. They'd run off with their tails between their legs, and it would be some time before they gathered enough energy to reform themselves.

"Gabby," Tristan said, kneeling beside her.

She held up her hand, holding the knight at bay. "Give me a minute…"

Delving inside herself, she pushed the dark coil of power back into its box, and to her surprise, it went willingly. She didn't know what it meant, but for now, she was still herself, and she was glad. The power hadn't corrupted her, but she was drained to the point she wanted to curl up in bed for a week. She was so sleeping in tomorrow.

Isobel knelt beside Nye's prone body, her hands stroking his face and hair as tears fell from her eyes.

"Will he come back?" she was asking Alex. "Is he dead?"

Her brother shook his head. "He'll wake in a few hours." He wiped at the rune carved into the vampire's chest. "He's already starting to heal. See?"

"Are you sure?" she asked. "I couldn't handle it if he…"

Gabby reached out for Tristan's hand, and the

knight helped her to her feet. "Get Nye back to the mansion," she said, wincing as her muscles started to ache. "I need to have a look around."

"Are you sure?" he asked, holding her tightly. "You're—"

"I'll be fine," she interrupted. "I've still got plenty of juice. Besides, there might be something here that can help us. The Unhallowed aren't gone for good...just for now. We need more... Tonight was just dumb luck." Really, it was the stupidest luck they'd ever had, and they'd done a lot of stupid things in the last year. She didn't have enough fingers to count them on—there were that many.

Tristan didn't seem convinced. "Someone should stay with you. Just in case."

She nodded as the adrenaline in her body began to wear off and her nerve endings started to vibrate. "Perhaps."

"Are you okay, Gabby?" Isobel asked, finally glancing up from her panicked vigil over Nye.

"Yes," she replied. "Go. Take him home. I'll be there soon."

It was an odd sight to see Alex carrying Nye's body in his arms. Having known Alex since she'd first moved to Ashburton when she was a teenager, it was almost comical. He'd been a weedy weakling back then but had grown into a handsome, muscled gardener. Now he was something else, of course.

As Izzy disappeared with the men, she turned to

Tristan, commanding him to make sure they were alone. They'd literally caused quite a stir in the otherwise serene countryside and didn't want to attract any unwanted attention. Especially not when she felt so terrible.

Sighing, she leaned against the standing stone behind her and calmed her thoughts. They finally had a short reprieve so they could catch their breath and find a way to end the Unhallowed for good.

At least something had gone right today.

CHAPTER 20

Gabby lingered within the stone circle, the darkness almost absolute.

Raising her hands, she flicked a small spark from her fingertips and ignited what was left of the torches the Unhallowed had used in their ritual. Without the other elements of their tainted magic, they were just big sticks.

Light flooded the circle, and Gabby began her search, feeling out the remains of their spell work. Her fingertips brushed the Blood Stone where they'd found Nye, and it was here she felt the ragged edges of the tether they'd used to bind him to the ley lines. She didn't know this magic, but one thing she did understand was it had been agony for her friend.

There was another surprise for the night. Admitting Nye was her friend. Duty and honour to Regulus had driven her to stay and help the spy take her lover's place as leader of the London vampires, but somehow, the cocky vampire had grown on her...and it had nothing to do with Izzy's feelings for the guy.

Even if Nye wasn't part of the equation, the Unhallowed were a problem. A *witch* problem, which made it her jurisdiction.

Gabby didn't need the power of a coven behind her to fight a power like this...she was her own coven. She was as strong as ten matriarchs combined. No, she was a lone wolf in her world. Her mind would be enough.

"Nothin' stirs," Tristan said, emerging from the darkness. "If you intend to commune with the ley lines, you're safe to do so. I will watch over you until you return."

She nodded and settled beside the Blood Stone, crossing her legs and placing her palms against the earth. The soil was churned up with footprints and splashes of Nye's blood, but it wouldn't matter. The earth was all around.

It was in the sky, the wind, the soil, the water, and the plants that grew within it. It was even inside the humans and animals that lived upon it. Everywhere she looked, there was a piece of the earth she was tasked with protecting in the Celestine's stead. Communing with it was second nature to all witches, but she'd never considered delving into the ley lines themselves. She hadn't even thought it was something she could do...but a lot of things had changed her mind about what was possible.

Gabby slipped through the veil without resistance, the air shimmering around her and dissolving into the ice that told her she was in the spirit realm. The current of the ley line was all around pulling her in different directions—neither up nor down, left or right —all laws of gravity ceasing to be.

The Unhallowed had linked themselves to this place by tapping into its energy. Theoretically, she should be able to reach inside their memories and sift through them. They'd left rather abruptly and had no time to cover their tracks. If she were lucky, she'd be able to find out their end game...and a way to stop them for good. *Fingers crossed.*

Reaching out with her mind, Gabby let her earth sense meld with the ley line stream. Almost instantly, she was sucked under, spiralling out of control. She tried to struggle as panic began to overcome her. If she drowned in the earth's energy, where would she end up? There was no way of telling.

Gabby spun out of control and gasped as everything stopped, and a warm light lit up a strange room in front of her. Before her, a fire popped merrily in the hearth, her skirts heavy and coarse against her legs as she knelt before someone...a woman in matching clothing. She was older than Gabby—perhaps forty or fifty. Her curly hair was streaked with grey and pulled back into a severe braid, and her lips were pinched, giving away her irritation.

She stared up at the woman and blinked hard. Whose body had the witch spirits dumped her into?

"We would have discovered your duplicity soon enough," the woman said with an air of disappointment. "You are chosen, Eleanor. You will lead us out of the darkness and into a brighter future. All you have to do is lure your vampire lover into the woods and carve the rune into his flesh."

Eleanor! This must be the events leading up to the moment Nye killed her original human form, but what did the woman mean about using his flesh? Why was Nye so important to their cause? He was just a regular vampire...wasn't he? This must be an important moment if the earth was forcing her to witness it.

"As you command, mother," she heard Eleanor say as if she was speaking the words herself. "It shall be done."

"The Unhallowed will rejoice," the woman said, smiling widely. "You will bear the fruit of our salvation."

This was getting weird. Bearing fruit and salvation had an ominous tone to it, and it had nothing to do with being flung back to the Middle Ages.

The scene shifted, and she glanced back over her shoulder at the man who followed her through the wood. Nye. He smiled, his expression full of love. Snow had begun to fall around them, the flakes beginning to flutter thicker and faster, coating the earth white as they walked.

When they reached a clearing, Eleanor dropped his hand and pushed Nye back against a tree, pressing her lips against his. Gross! Gabby had no control over what was happening and had to ride it out as the pair began to get really into it. How was she going to look Nye in the eye and not puke now?

He kissed Eleanor/Gabby with all the passion he could muster, sliding his tongue against hers. Gabby felt the magic rising in her as Nye lost himself in the kiss, and she shoved him back, twisting her power around his throat and squeezing.

Gagging, the vampire stumbled, clutching at his neck. "What have you done?"

"The Unhallowed will suffer your presence no longer," she declared, pushing him again, and he fell backward into the snow as her will wove through his body, slowing his movements.

Eleanor straddled him, pulled out the blade she'd stashed underneath her cloak—the blade her mother had given her to carry out her destiny—and pressed it against his forehead.

As the metal cut into the flesh of his forehead, he hissed at her, but she ignored his pitiful moaning and continued carving the rune into his skin.

"Such an unfortunate life," she crooned as she worked her magic. "So much pain. I will take it away. I will deliver you, Nye. I promise."

She began to speak in the strange language of the

witches, and the symbol she'd cut into his forehead began to do its work, binding his soul.

"Eleanor—"

She/Gabby was so intent on her work she didn't sense the moment when a hand fisted in her hair and dragged her off Nye's body. The spell was severed before it could be completed, and she cried out in rage. *No!*

Staring up at her assailant, her mouth dropped open.

Regulus!

With his hand fisted in her hair, he forced her to the ground, snow soaking her knees. He was too strong, and struggling only made the Roman twist her hair more painfully.

It wasn't the Regulus Gabby had known. This was Regulus four hundred years in the past...long before she was even born. Despite being stuffed into Eleanor's memories, she felt a desperate longing at the sight of her dead love. He didn't know it was her, he wasn't really here, but he was so close... His presence had torn her soul away from Eleanor—the vision had become more lifelike than she'd realised—and she was a witness once more.

"You know what you need to do, brother," he said to Nye. With his free hand, he drew a sword and offered it to the vampire, hilt first.

Nye stood and took the sword, his gaze meeting hers. He was hesitating...

"The love you feel is false," Regulus said. "End her and you will end your misery."

Gabby felt the air began to thicken as Eleanor reached for her power...and Nye didn't falter. He raised the sword and struck with all his strength.

The next thing Eleanor saw after Nye had severed her head from her body was the world Gabby now stood in. The spirit realm. She felt the tug of the ley line, a different line...and only one this time. Voices began to carry on the current rushing past her as her life slipped away. Something had bid Eleanor's spirit to stay after her death. The Unhallowed? Most likely, which would mean there had been wraiths in the coven for longer than four hundred years. Did they consider the darker spirit energy as their birthright?

The voices became louder, crooning their lament to Eleanor.

We will find it. We want it. It will be ours. We will have it. It is our birthright. We will have our destiny. The Keeping Place awaits...

The whispers were everywhere, whipping around her like spectres. She whirled, trying to grasp hold of the voices, but they were slippery and ran through her fingers like ash.

What was Eleanor meant to do that day? What was she trying to do now, *tonight*, with Nye? If the stone circle wasn't the Keeping Place, then where was it?

Gabby!

The unknown voice practically slapped her in the

face with its warning, and her eyes snapped open. She was back in the physical world, her stomach rolling at the sudden shift in planes. Her gaze collided with Tristan, who was standing over her with a look of anger plastered on his face. His eyes were swirling, turning black as he allowed his vampirism to override his human compassion.

She scrambled backward with a gasp, her back hitting the Blood Stone. This wasn't him. He'd never… unless something *had* happened the night Eleanor attacked him.

She'd bewitched Tristan!

It explained a great deal about the sudden removal of the barrier around the mansion. She must've compelled the knight to kill Nye's witch and lure Isobel outside where she could get to her. What an epic bitch.

"Tristan, listen to me," she said, holding her hand up, readying herself to unleash her power on the vampire. "You're under Eleanor's spell. This isn't you. I know it isn't you. You'd never hurt me or any of your friends."

"You don't know me, Gabby," he said, his eyes beginning to change as he let his fangs grow in. "We're in this because of circumstance. Nothin' more."

"Then why hurt me? What's that got to do with circumstance?"

He faltered for a split second before advancing again. "I have to kill you," he said. "You're a problem. You're in the way."

"Don't make me hurt you," she declared, feeling her power rise. "Back off."

"It will be over before you even feel anythin'"

"What do they want, Tristan?" she asked, stalling him. "What do the Unhallowed want with Nye?"

He faltered, his brow creasing. "Don't you know?" He raised his hand and began outlining a shape on his forehead with the tip of his finger. When he reached the star, he smiled as he traced each point.

"Resurrection?" Gabby asked with a gasp. "What's Nye got to do with that?"

Tristan had stopped listening and bared his fangs. She had to strike now before it was too late.

As the knight lunged, she unleashed her power, throwing everything she had left against the thousand-year-old vampire. His body came to a halt mere inches from her face, his eyes wide with shock, and she twisted her hand around. His neck snapped with an audible crack, and he fell to the ground before her, dead to the world.

Holy hell!

Her heart hammered in her chest as she pressed her back against the Blood Stone, the night stretching out around the lonely scene. A witch cowering against an ancient slab of bluestone with a temporarily dead vampire at her feet.

She had to get out of here. He'd wake soon enough and still be under Eleanor's spell. The wraith wasn't dead, so her poison would remain until Gabby removed it. She had to get him back to the mansion.

Pushing to her feet, she grasped his ankles and began dragging Tristan from the stone circle. Her muscles were going to hate her in the morning.

CHAPTER 21

Dawn was lightening the horizon when Gabby finally parked the car in the mansion's garage.

Pulling out her cell phone, she dialled Alex's number, and he answered almost immediately.

"Gabby?" came his voice. "Where are you?"

"Alex," she said, her hands trembling. "I need you to help me with Tristan. I'm in the garage."

"What happened?" came his fevered reply.

"Tristan… He was compelled by Eleanor…"

"Are you… Is he…"

"He'll be fine," she said, glancing at his comatose body in the back seat. "But he's currently unconscious…and I don't have super strength. Truthfully, I'm beat."

"Stay where you are," he said. "I'm on my way down."

When Alex appeared, she was surprised when he pulled her into his arms and hugged her tightly.

"Are you okay?" he asked. "Those were some epic skills you showed off tonight."

"Yeah. I'm just tired, I guess. Is Nye awake yet?" she asked as Alex let her go so he could open the back door to retrieve Tristan.

"Not yet. Izzy is with him now. His chest is healing, but it's weird…" He dragged the comatose vampire out and hauled him over his shoulder like a bag of potting mix. You could take the gardener out of the garden…

"What's weird?"

"It should've healed by now," Alex went on as they moved into the mansion. "The rune that crazy wraith sliced into him…Izzy's worried."

"They were using some pretty heavy magic," Gabby said. "Dark stuff. It could just be taking time to work out of his system."

"I hope so," he grumbled. "My sister says she loves him. And I warned him if he hurt her again… I will kill him, Gabby. If he does anything to hurt a hair on Izzy's head, I'll rip his off."

"I don't doubt it," she replied. "But save it as a last resort, huh?"

Alex didn't complain further and carried the unconscious Tristan upstairs to the knight's room with Gabby in tow. Looked like she'd have to pay Nye a visit too before she could finally fall into bed.

When she stepped into Tristan's room, she raised an eyebrow at the scene before her. She hadn't seen his room before, and she was certain no one ever had. It was sparsely furnished, the bed simple and the walls free of any adornment. The vampire was a strange one, loyal and devout to whatever cause he was fighting for. As Alex set him down on the bed, she wondered if all of this was an extension of his lingering humanity. From what she'd heard Tristan had spent most of his life marching across Europe and what were now Turkey and the Middle East on the Crusades. Which one, she wasn't sure since there had been several.

"Can you do this now?" Alex asked as she sat beside the knight. "You look like you need a good sleep."

"I have to do this now," she replied. "If he wakes up and is still under Eleanor's control, then we'd just have another mess to deal with. Besides, he's a good guy. He doesn't deserve to be used like this."

He stood beside her and placed his hand on her shoulder. "What happened out there?"

"Lots of things. Tristan tried to attack me, so I must be close to figuring out the Unhallowed's endgame."

"He *attacked* you?"

"Give me some credit, Alex," she said with a tired smile. "I did break his neck with a flick of the wrist."

"*Badass*," he said with a grin.

Shaking her head, she turned her attention to Tristan. Focusing her power, she delved into the vampire's mind. Technically, he was dead, or in a really weird form of stasis, so she was able to unravel Eleanor's compulsion with little to no effort on her part. If he had been conscious, he would've fought back at the intrusion, making it annoying as hell in her current condition.

Opening her eyes, she sighed, her body beginning to tremble as her power reached its ultimate limit.

"He should be okay, but he'll need to be watched," she declared, her bones aching something fierce. "We need to get one of Nye's Six here."

"Nye's Six?" Alex asked.

"Reed," she replied. "Get Reed and I'll invite him in. Nye and Tristan seemed to trust the guy, and right now, we need help." They were stretched thin when all of them were in commission, and now that Nye and Tristan were both down, she was it.

"I have Nye's cell," he said. "Izzy found it in her room before. I'll arrange for this Reed guy to come as soon as he can."

"Thanks."

"You sure you're okay?"

She nodded and pushed to her feet. "I've been through worse. An extra hour on my feet won't hurt me."

Leaving Alex to arrange Reed's arrival, she shuffled through the mansion to Isobel's room. Knowing her friend, she would've commanded her brother to take the vampire there. It's what she would've done if it were Regulus. A familiar place where she could protect the man she loved.

As she hauled herself up the stairs to the other

wing of the house, she felt a pang of longing for the dead Roman. How she wished he were here. If anyone knew what to do with unabashed certainty, it was Regulus, but all Gabby had right now was the hope that some of his ruthlessness had rubbed off on her. She'd need it in the final showdown with the Unhallowed.

Eleanor was going down, one way or another.

Isobel sat on her bed with Nye's hand firmly wedged in hers.

She studied the vampire's face while he lay dead, healing from his self-inflicted stab wound to the heart. He was still and serene, his hand icy in hers. She hadn't realised exactly how cold his body was compared to hers. They'd touched before, kissed even, but she'd been too wrapped up in her feelings to take note.

She memorised each line of his face, including his scar, and started to become concerned with how long he'd been out. It'd been several hours since they'd returned from the stone circle, and while Nye's chest had almost healed, he was still some place faraway.

"Hey."

She glanced up at the sound of Gabby's voice. "You're back!"

"How is he?" the witch asked, venturing into the room.

"Still out," she replied. "I'm beginning to worry..."

Gabby nodded and pulled down the blanket Isobel had placed over Nye. For a long moment, the witch studied the mark on his chest, her fingers probing the angry-looking skin.

"Why isn't it going away?" Isobel asked after a moment.

"I'm not sure. There was some heavy-duty power flowing through him... That had to have some consequences."

"It's just slowed his healing, right?"

Her friend shrugged. "It's possible. All we can do right now is wait."

"He stabbed himself in the heart," she said. "How can he come back from that?"

"Only a stake can kill him," Gabby explained. "Wood or silver. The dagger was made out of steel, and he knew the right place to strike so his body could repair itself. If he were gone..."

"If he were gone?"

"His body would desiccate."

She'd seen it before when her brother killed Aed. Of course, Nye was still here.

"Does it usually take this long?" she asked.

Gabby shrugged. "I suppose a hole in a heart is a little more complicated than most mortal wounds. All we can do is wait."

Isobel glanced at Nye and tightened her grip on his hand, willing him to wake while her mind went back to the events of the night. Everything had happened so fast...

She'd stood right behind Gabby as the witch ripped the earth apart around them. Full-on tore it to shreds and put them into the eye of a tornado...but then there were the Unhallowed. She'd been powerless in that moment, watching the six women flicker from solid human form into storm clouds of their own. The things she'd seen in the past few months defied everything that was logical. Then there was the man who lay before her, dead but not... Four hundred years and just as many lifetimes under his belt, and here she was, a baby compared to his understanding of the world.

"What were they?" she asked, shoving away her doubts. "Those women? I know you said they're wraiths, but... They looked human one second, then..."

"Wraiths are nothing like I've ever seen, either," Gabby replied. "And I've seen some crazy shit. Neither living nor dead, they assume human forms and feed off the power of the ley lines to prolong their lives. Without it, their bodies decay and their souls are lost in a supernatural limbo for eternity."

"The ley lines under the stone circle? That's why they needed them so bad?"

The witch nodded. "Now that I've seen and felt what they can do, I'm fairly certain they move around, and as one line is depleted, they find another so the one they fed off can grow again. A constant push and pull with the other side."

"What a life," she drawled. "Clinging to life like a leech."

"I don't think the stone circle was the Keeping Place," Gabby said, lost in thought.

"But the map..." Isobel began to argue.

"Just led us to their ritual."

"Then what has this Keeping Place got to do with Nye?"

Gabby shrugged. "Whatever is in the Keeping Place might be something that will give the Unhallowed enough power to not have to use the ley lines anymore. An unlimited power source, maybe... It's just a guess, but the memories the earth showed me pointed toward something they were looking for." She frowned, remembering the matriarch's words. "She said Eleanor would bear the fruit of their salvation."

"That doesn't sound whacked at all," Izzy drawled.

"What do you think?" Gabby asked.

"Me?" Her eyes widened. Someone was asking her what she thought? *Finally!*

The witch shrugged. "Any clue is a good clue."

"Well," she said, glancing at Nye, whose eyes were still closed. "Bearing fruit is usually a fertility reference in ancient text. They could be growing something, or..."

"A baby?" Gabby asked, curling her nose. "A wraith baby? Impossible."

"Why was Eleanor so desperate for Nye to be a part of finding this Keeping Place? Was it just revenge, or do you think…"

"The only thing more absurd than a wraith baby is a vampire one."

"Then maybe something about Nye is part of a map or key?" she threw out, hoping something was right.

"We could be speculating all day," Gabby replied with a rather large yawn. "Let's wait for Nye to recover first. He might know more seeing as he had a chance to talk to Eleanor. He knew he had to sever himself from the ley line, which was why he…" She gestured to the dead vampire.

Isobel scowled and turned back to Nye, taking his hand once more. She hated the fact Eleanor had her claws in him at all. Jealousy and anger rose inside her, and for the first time, she said what she was feeling about the vampire who'd stolen her heart. Stolen it without even trying, she might add. "Despite everything that's happened, the things he's done, who he is, and what he is, I love him. *I love Nye.*"

"I know," Gabby replied. "I know."

"What a fickle thing the heart is," she murmured.

"You'll get your chance to tell him, Izzy," her friend said. "Don't doubt that."

There was a soft knock on the door, and Alex appeared. "Gabby, Reed is here."

The witch nodded and rose to her feet. "I'll be right down."

"Reed?" Isobel asked. "Anything to worry about?"

"Nope. Just one last thing to do before I get to sleep the day and night away," she replied. "Tristan needs watching, and Nye trusts Reed, so in he comes."

Once Gabby had left, Isobel turned back to Nye, casting Reed to the back of her mind. Another vampire in the mansion! If Nye trusted him, then she was content to follow suit and care for the one who mattered the most.

Nye still hadn't stirred, but his skin had healed over entirely now, so she pulled the covers up over his chest to keep him warm...even though he probably didn't need it. Yet another thing she wasn't used to about his kind.

Curling up beside him, she closed her eyes, relieved he was back in the mansion—away from the wicked Unhallowed—and in her bed, right where she wanted him all along.

CHAPTER 22

Nye had died many times as a vampire and had always come back eventually.

He'd had his neck snapped, his throat slit, a knife or two shoved through his gut—such was the life of the leader of the Six—but there was something different about this time.

Usually, awareness came back to his body abruptly, like someone had thrown a switch. But this time, he felt like he was rising to the surface of a tepid pool of water, his limbs heavy and unable to move.

He still felt the echo of power that had flown through him, linking his body to the Unhallowed...and Eleanor. Was that the reason he was having trouble coming back? And what exactly was he coming back to? They shouldn't have come. Gabby, Tristan, Alex... *Isobel*. They should have let him die.

No matter his suffering or how long it took for them to end him—*they shouldn't have come.*

He'd locked eyes with Isobel and plunged the dagger into his heart, just so... It was her horrified expression he saw as the life fled his body, the last image that he took into the darkness.

The Unhallowed's link had been severed from the ley lines, and he'd died yet another vampire death. It had all felt so *real*.

Eleanor had gotten into his head before, taunting him in what should have been a dreamless sleep, and projected her image of the night he'd gone to the off-license. Reflected in the glass door of the refrigerator like a warning. Now he understood that she had been there.

When his eyes opened, he instantly knew he was at the mansion...in Isobel's bed. *Thank God*. Gabby must've been able to overwhelm the wraiths after he'd severed their link.

"Isobel," he said, his voice bursting forth in a painful rasp.

"I'm here," she said, her face coming into focus. "You're safe."

"What happened?"

"Gabby was able to send the wraiths packing after you..." She glanced away. "They're still out there."

He closed his eyes, knowing that they were pretty much back at square one. His sacrifice had been for nothing...but Isobel...she seemed to be awake, so the curse had remained lifted.

"Here," she murmured, offering him a glass.

He sat up and took it, his gaze focusing on the contents. Blood. She shouldn't have to give him this. She shouldn't have to be here... He shouldn't have made her stay the day she turned up looking for Alex. He'd ruined her future. Her safe, happy future.

"Nye?" she prodded, her voice sounding faraway.

He stood, his body shaking with the effort of containing his anger. Not at her, never at her. He was furious with himself for letting the Unhallowed get their hands on her in the first place. All of this was his fault.

"*I didn't want to be saved!*" he roared, throwing the glass across the room.

She flinched and sucked in a shallow breath as it shattered against the wall, blood trickling down the paintwork.

"I sacrificed myself to save—" He stopped mid-sentence, nostrils flaring as he seethed.

"Say it, Nye," she whispered. "Tell me what you want me to hear. Break my heart one last time. I know it's a lie. *I know*."

"After everything, you still believe—" He grimaced, shaking his head. "It doesn't matter how I feel. Loving me will only see you killed or worse."

"There's something worse than death?" she scoffed, rising to her feet.

"Go," he said, casting his gaze away. "Go as far and as fast as you can. The Unhallowed are my problem."

"I won't leave you!" she cried, standing beside him. "*I can't.* It's impossible."

"*Get out!*" he roared, turning to face her with black eyes. "I don't want you, Isobel. You are not welcome here. *Get out.*"

Tears began to stream down her face, and she shook her head defiantly. "*Liar.*"

"Isobel, please..."

"I love you, Nye," she declared, grasping his face in her warm hands. "I love you. Don't ask me how the hell it happened, but it did. Just like that."

"Just like that," he echoed, her words slicing into him...deeper than Eleanor's dagger ever could.

"See?" she prodded, begging him for a response. "I couldn't leave you even if I tried. It's impossible."

He didn't deserve the conviction behind her words. He'd done nothing but hurt her, and yet here she was —a human woman with a pure heart—fighting for him? A vampire who'd committed countless horrors?

"I need..." he began, his gaze dropping. That's when he saw the marks on his bare chest.

The rune was still present. It was healed over but still there. He could see it was fading and would disappear eventually, but the fact it was there at all had him worried.

"I need to clean up," he muttered, ignoring the look of disappointment on Isobel's face.

"Yeah," she whispered, taking a step back.

She wanted him to tell her he loved her, and he

did, but... Turning, he strode across the room, leaving her standing there on the verge of tears. If he remained beside her in the state he was...it was dangerous. He needed to gather himself before he could face that emotion.

Closing himself in her bathroom, he grasped the edge of the basin and tried to hold himself together. Getting angry wouldn't solve anything. His knuckles began to turn white, but he didn't pull away until the marble started to crack underneath the force of his restrained fury.

Ripping his ruined shirt open, he inspected the symbol the wraiths had carved into his chest. It had faded even more since the minute before, still much slower than usual, but what did he expect? The Unhallowed had marked him for something bigger than revenge for taking Eleanor's human life.

What they were and what they'd become were two different things.

He stood in the shower for what felt like an age, scrubbing the dried blood from his skin, but no matter how much soap he applied to the cloth, the rune still wouldn't fade fast enough. He was well and truly clean despite the remnants of Eleanor's handiwork, so he turned off the spray of water, dried off, and dressed before finally emerging into the bedroom in a waft of steam.

Isobel was on her hands and knees, cleaning up the mess he'd made when he'd thrown the glass across the room, and he felt his anxiety fall away, only to be replaced by longing. Loving a human, huh? It was going to be one hell of a ride.

"Isobel," he murmured, curling his hands around her wrists and urging her to her feet.

"But I've got to clean this up," she complained, holding back tears.

"Fuck the mess," he said, tugging her toward him.

"Nye, please..." she said, trying to untangle herself from his grasp. She'd taken his earlier reaction as a rejection—that much was clear.

"I've made so many mistakes with you," he began, rubbing his hands up and down her arms. "I should've let you go home that day..."

"But—"

"Shh," he murmured, interrupting what was no doubt a complaint. "What's done is done, and I can't take any of it back. The curse is gone, the Unhallowed are running scared, but..."

"But?" she asked, her eyes still watering.

Her body trembled underneath his touch as he moved his hands to her face, cupping her flushed cheeks in his palms. "Love isn't something I've felt," he admitted. "Not a love like this. I'm not sure how..."

"Do you think I am?" she asked with a sigh. "I don't know shit about it, either."

"You knew when to say it," he replied. "And when to fight for it."

"And what about now?"

"Now…" he began, drawing in a sharp breath. "I'm yours, Isobel…but I think you already knew that."

"We can argue all day and night about who belongs to who," she whispered, her gaze lowering to his lips. "Or you could just kiss me and seal the deal."

Hoping the third time was a charm, he lowered his lips to hers and kissed her softly. He wasn't prepared for the wave of emotion that swept over him as he held her close. It smashed into him with surprising force, his newly repaired heart swelling.

When it became too much for him to handle, he tore his lips from hers and wrapped his arms around her, cradling her body against his like she was the most precious thing in the world.

"Knowing you, I'm sure you've been up all night," he murmured against her hair. "It's your turn to rest, dear Isobel."

"I can't go to sleep now," she argued. "All I want to do is kiss you some more."

He smiled, relishing the recklessness of their affection. "We'll have plenty of time for that, but for now, please get some rest. I can feel how tired you are."

"What do you mean by that?" she asked, pulling away from him. "Is that another vampire thing?"

"No," he replied, leading her toward the bed. "It's an observational thing. Nothing supernatural about it."

She practically fell into bed, giving up her charade of wakefulness. "*Smartass.*"

He wrapped her up in the quilt and lay beside her,

his front against her back with the material wedged between them. There was another hurdle in their cross-species relationship. The fire and ice that was their body temperatures.

"Nye?"

"Yeah?"

"Are you really okay?"

He hesitated, not knowing how to answer her. He was beginning to feel pretty damn fine, but the rune was still marking his skin.

"It's been a really long night," he replied. "Strange, fucked up, and totally psycho. I'll be fine with a little rest...and so will you."

She sighed, nestling back into him. "I want to believe you," she murmured, sounding sleepy. "But you have to make me a promise."

"Anything."

"No more secrets."

He closed his eyes, and not knowing if that was a promise he could keep, gave her the answer she wanted. "No more secrets."

Isobel seemed satisfied with his answer and began to settle in his arms. He listened with all his vampire senses for the moment she fell asleep, knowing that he didn't have a moment to lose in getting the upper hand with the Unhallowed. He had to seek out Tristan and make sure the knight was rid of the compulsion Eleanor put on him, and once that was done, begin to plan for the showdown of the century.

Isobel was his now, and he would do anything to keep her safe. He loved her and she loved him, and that was worth fighting for. If the London underworld crumbled and his throne was taken from underneath his ass, it wouldn't matter one bit...as long as she was with him.

Her heart rate slowed and her breathing became shallow as sleep finally took her away, reenergising her tired body. Slipping from the bed, he took one last look at her innocent features. He didn't know when things had changed from innocent flirtation to love, but the most important thing was that he felt it now. Between the four of them—Gabby, Alex, Tristan, and himself—she would be safe from anyone or anything that would do her harm.

Leaving her to rest, Nye ghosted into the study where he found Tristan slumped in the armchair beside the fireplace.

"Are you still compelled?" he asked as the knight glanced up.

"Gabby removed it after I tried to kill her," he replied. "What about you?"

"We've got a problem," he snarled, ignoring the vampire's unwanted concern over his health.

"Which problem are you talkin' about because we've got a lot of them?"

"The Unhallowed are coming back for me, and I will not let them get their hands on Isobel again."

"What do you propose? With the Six out handlin'

the vampires and Gabby's power at almost nothin', we don't have much firepower. We need time to regroup."

Nye squared his jaw, his lip pulling into a sneer. "I will do whatever it takes. *Whatever it takes.* If I have to leave a trail of bodies behind me, then so be it. The Unhallowed will *burn.*"

EPILOGUE

The sound of scratching echoed through the still graveyard, the six-hundred-year-old church standing tall in the gloom of twilight.

Eleanor's fingers dug into the earth, feeling for the place where the earth energy leaked to the surface. She was so tired, so hungry for the power that would keep her from slipping back into the otherworld. Four hundred years she'd been clawing at the bottom rungs of life, searching for the ultimate revenge. *Resurrection.* Not just hers...all of them.

That bitch Gabrielle Cohen had banished her to the far reaches of the spirit realm, stealing her power and casting her sisters back into the void. The witch was so clueless. She didn't even realise what she'd done! They would all pay—Gabrielle and Nye the most. When the coven was resurrected, they would beg for mercy.

Dirt clung underneath her fingernails, the life her

five sisters had given her so she could claw her way back into the world of the living rejoicing as she found it. *The ley line.*

She smiled, her eyes beginning to glow with white fire as the ley line responded to her, filling her veins with the intoxicating energy of the earth. Her power was slowly being restored, her life force growing stronger with every passing moment, and soon, the generations of ancient Unhallowed witches would join her.

"Eleanor."

She glanced up at the spirit before her and knelt, her knees pressing into the damp earth.

"Matriarch," she replied, bowing her head.

"Explain to me why our coven still languishes in the otherworld?"

The spirit was the matriarch of the Unhallowed, the voice that spoke for them all. Eleanor was the matriarch's heir, and the only one trusted enough to carry out this task, a weapon to be wielded in the war for resurrection. She answered to the higher power of the matriarch...her mother.

"I failed, but I *have* planted the seed," Eleanor replied. "It may not be me who bares the fruit of our salvation, but it shall be borne."

"This is our last chance at survival, child," the matriarch snarled. "If you fail, you doom us all to oblivion."

Eleanor smiled, knowing that it was only a matter

of time before they got what they wanted. *The seed had been planted,* and now was the time to be patient and regain her strength. The time was coming when she'd need to strike, and Gabrielle Cohen would not get in her way a second time.

"You have nothing to fear, Mother," she said, smiling up at the apparition. "Their love will be their undoing...*and our salvation.*"

Nye, Gabby and Isobel's story will be continued in book six, The Keeping Place... coming soon.

THE KEEPING PLACE
(The Witch Hunter Saga #6)

Vampires and conspiracies. Witches and curses. It's just another day to the London Vampires...

Nye Saer is a vampire with a big problem.

Rescued from the clutches of The Unhallowed, he's battered and weary, and his power is at an all time low. With rebelling vampires on one side, a coven of psychopathic wraiths on the other, and trouble at home, he doesn't know where to turn.

The Unhallowed are still out there and they're coming back. Not just for him this time, but also the woman he loves.

Gabby Cohen is one of the most powerful witches alive. She's battled spirits, dark witches, curses, founding vampires, werewolves and fae hybrids. She's seen it all, hasn't she?

But when she finds what the Unhallowed have hidden in the Keeping Place, all Gabby's strength may not be enough to stop them.

The mismatched group of vampires, witches and humans are on borrowed time, and as they search desperately for a way to fight back, they stumble on the biggest conspiracy of all.

A conspiracy that began in 1603...

***The Keeping Place** concludes the story begun in the Urban Fantasy series, **The Witch Hunter Saga** — In a world remade, the London vampires must find their way out of chaos...without losing everything to a bunch of blood-thirsty witches.*

The Keeping Place is OUT NOW!!!

ABOUT NICOLE

Nicole R. Taylor is the author of the bestselling Urban Fantasy series, The Witch Hunter Saga.

She writes about vampires with complexes, insane witches, super heroes, post-apocalyptic warriors and samurai sword wielding women...all from a desk in a country town near Melbourne, Australia.

Follow Nicole Online:

Website: www.nicolertaylorwrites.com
Twitter: twitter.com/nicole_noir
Facebook: facebook.com/nrtaylorwrites
Newsletter: www.nicolertaylorwrites.com/newsletter
Email: nicole.this.is@gmail.com

www.ingramcontent.com/pod-product-compliance
Lightning Source LLC
Chambersburg PA
CBHW030804200726
48285CB00014B/596